WILD WEDDINGS

THE MCALLISTER BROTHERS SERIES BOOK 4

CRICKET ROHMAN

Cover design & interior formatting by: Sweet 'N Spicy Designs

ISBN: 978-1-7355672-4-2
Ebook ISBN: 978-1-7355672-5-9

NOVELS BY CRICKET ROHMAN

Saving Madeline

Standalone Contemporary Fiction

The McAllister Brothers Series

Romantic Western Adventures

Colorado Takedown

Montana Countdown

Wyoming Sundown

Wild Weddings

The Creative Hearts Sweet Romance Series

Creative Women Novellas

Phoebe's Photo Fetish

Anna's Animal House

Caitlin's Cow Wash

Tina's Tasty Tours

The Lindsey Lark Series

Fiction with Elements of Romance & Mystery

Wanted: An Honest Man

Letters, Lovers, & Lies

Hit The Road, Jake!

The Fantasy Maker Series

Contemporary Adventures

Forever Island

Winter's Blush

ACKNOWLEDGMENTS

I would like to say thank you to:

My readers. Because of you, I keep writing.

Jerry Gallegos, my husband, my cowboy, my go-to ranch and horse-training consultant.

Jaycee DeLorenzo, my amazing, wonderful formatter/cover designer who's always there when I need her.

My talented editor, Michelle Kowalski, for her attention to details and keen sense of story.

Horses — especially the Spanish Barbs I've come to know. Their beauty and strength is a constant inspiration.

This book is dedicated to:
Hard working ranch families,
Animal lovers,
Foster parents,
And
Wedding planners.

THE GAME CAMERA, GOOD & PLENTY, AND THE WINTER WONDERLAND

CHAPTER ONE

ALICE

I rang a small bell to announce that breakfast was about to be served. This was not just any random meal; this would be our last time breaking bread together for quite a while. Wanting everything to be extra special, I enlisted my oldest son's help. Troy was by far the best chef in the family. He loved to create gourmet meals and always added something noteworthy to simple meals, even breakfast. He didn't get that trait from me.

Delicious smells floated through the air of the large kitchen. The table, set in the center, could accommodate all eight of us and left plenty of room around the edges for the pets: one cat, two kittens, one dog, one puppy, and a coyote pup named Shadow. The kitchen was their favorite place. Often, five-year-old Billy accompanied the animals, but today the critters appeared first.

When the adults had yet to arrive even after I rang my bell, I called out to my youngest son, who I could always rely on.

"Trace? Breakfast is ready. Fetch your dad, help him into his wheelchair, and bring him to the head of the table."

"I got this, Mom. We'll be right there."

Hannah, Trace's gal, and Ivy, Troy's, entered the kitchen together. It did seem that my sons made good choices, but, of course, it was too soon to know for sure. And then there was Billy, the five-year-old child who called Troy daddy, Ivy mommy, and me grandma. That just didn't sit well with me. There wasn't a single drop of McAllister blood in him. He was merely a foster child.

I greeted each family member, even the gals. The room buzzed with activity and conversation as serving dishes of bacon, pancakes, scrambled eggs, and toast were passed around.

Forks in hand, we were about to dig in when Kitchi stood, raised his arms toward the sky, and asked for a moment of silence.

"In your quiet mind, appreciate food, family, the earth, the oceans—anything that comes to you. Be thankful," he said.

With my head partially bowed, I snuck a few quick peeks. If anyone else was peeking, I never saw it. Billy had his head bowed and his little hands folded, and even the animals sat very still. All in all, a calm, stress-free moment washed over me. However, not wanting the delicious food to get cold, I broke the silence.

"Thank you, Kitchi. We can always count on you to remind us what is truly important."

I'd met Kitchi, Troy's right-hand man at The Lonely Horse Ranch, a mere two weeks ago on Christmas Eve. The man was not much of a talker. He spoke only when he felt it was necessary. So I questioned Troy to learn more about this Native American man who sat at my table. Yes, until all the paperwork was signed and recorded, I still claimed everything here as mine. Well, mine and Clint's.

"Mom, he is the wisest man I've ever known," Troy whispered. "He's part of the Algonquin tribe and has been with me since the first week Dad sent me to Montana to develop a property there."

The delicious breakfast disappeared quickly, but there was more. Troy set a beautiful coffee cake on the table.

"Are we having dessert?" Billy asked. "I never had dessert with breakfast. It looks yummy."

Trace stood up and announced that he was about to make a toast. "Here in Wyoming in the dead of winter, and I do mean dead, we've had the best of times . . . and some of the worst. But we did it together and we all survived. Here's to many more best of times together."

"Hear! Hear!"

"Right on!"

"Amen!"

"Can we eat the cake now?"

Oh, yes. We dove right into the coffee cake that Troy had baked earlier this morning. I couldn't recall putting so much food into my mouth in one sitting. Already I could feel a few extra pounds accumulating around my middle. I thought I might need to ride my horse more often when we got back to Golden, Colorado, where Clint and I lived.

From his wheelchair, my husband raised his glass. "I'd like to propose an orange juice toast to the new property owners, the unexpected winners of my winter challenge. I know they will develop this land into something special, commendable. Here's to Hannah and Ivy, the new owners, soon to be my daughters-in-law, and official members of the McAllister family."

Hannah blushed, and I could see Ivy taking slow, deep breaths. Both of their lives had changed drastically in a few action-packed months, though I still wanted to know more about the trouble at Troy's Lonely Horse Ranch and Ivy's captors. Perhaps they felt that the

Christmas season was not the time to rehash those danger-filled days. I vowed to eventually get every last detail.

"Don't forget to come up with a name for your ranch," Clint added. "The H-I Double M Ranch was just a name I made up on the spot when I realized I'd be awarding the ranch to the two of you."

"We've got some ideas but aren't ready to make anything official yet. Once we decide exactly what developments we will implement, we'll have a name." Hannah spoke with sweet confidence. I was fond of confidence, but sweet? Not so much.

I glanced toward Ivy wondering if she felt the same way. I could tell that she had something to say, though her words came slowly.

She sighed and then said, "Knowing our unusual circumstances, turning this land, the old cabin, and barn into a working ranch or business of some kind will be tricky, to say the least."

Well, it seemed she was a realist. And, perhaps, the gals would come to the conclusion that their ranch project would be next to impossible to create and maintain.

I couldn't resist adding, "And don't forget that we need to begin planning two weddings."

Ivy

I WASN'T sure that Alice liked the idea of us owning this wild and wooly property here in Wyoming. I lived in Montana and Hannah lived in a remote area of Colorado. To make our new venture successful, we'd need to spend quite a bit of time many miles from our homes and our men. Still, we were determined to turn this place into something that would help nature, animals, and maybe even humanity. The sky was the limit.

Hannah and Trace cleared the table. Alice insisted on doing the dishes. Anxious to return to Montana with Troy, Billy, and Shadow, I did not mingle for long with the kitchen crew. Instead, I chose to make sure we were all packed up and ready to make the drive home just as soon as those dishes were done. A little too much time with so many people under the same roof was a challenge for me; thus, I nibbled on small chocolate candies often. I found dark chocolate, the darker the better, quite calming.

My attention turned to Kitchi as I saw him hurrying across the living room, the look on his somber face slowing me down. We had a pretty good relationship. He helped me out of several jams with his strength and his wisdom. But now, as I looked at him, my curious side sensed something was different.

"You're quiet this morning, Kitchi. Is everything all right?"

My question got Troy's attention and he looked up from tending the woodstove as if waiting for the man's answer too.

"Quiet is my nature, Miss Ivy. And yes, so far, everything is all right."

My eyes met Troy's. What did that wise Native American man mean? We knew his simple words often carried a deeper, sometimes spiritual, or otherworldly meaning. If only he hadn't thrown in the words "so far." I didn't like what that implied. Only time would reveal more about our state of "all-rightness."

"Hannah, Miss Ivy. Since you own this property, I will address my question to you," Kitchi said. "Would you mind if I stayed here one more day?"

Hannah stood in the kitchen's doorway and looked directly at me. She shrugged. I shrugged too and answered, "Of course, Kitchi. Make yourself at home. After all, you mentioned back on Christmas Eve that you had people who will help us with our exciting, though daunting, endeavor."

"I will lock up when I depart."

"Okay. Sounds good." Maybe he just needed a day to be alone. He'd tolerated almost two weeks of joyful chaos here at the ranch cabin. That had to be tough on a guy like him. I was amazed that he'd stuck around for so long, but now, asking to stay longer didn't make much sense to me. Usually, Troy couldn't get him to leave his job at the ranch for even a day.

Turning my attention back to my tasks, I dashed around making certain nothing vital would be left behind. Between Billy—he'd become the keeper of the pets—and the animals, I had plenty of not-so-helpful assistants with my efforts.

With everyone but Kitchi leaving at the same time, preparation for our departure caused quite a commotion. Fortunately, last week the men spent a long day backtracking to pick up their trucks and horse trailers that they'd parked at the starting point of Clint's original challenge for them.

Finally, the caravan of vehicles was packed up, lined up, and ready to go, though everyone lingered outside their vehicles as if they didn't want to leave. I was more than ready to get this show on the road, so I broke the awkward silence.

"All's well that ends well, right?"

"Yes, ma'am," Clint added.

Alice said, "Though not unscathed, we all survived."

"And we had the best Christmas in the whole wide world," Billy said as he beamed with joy.

"And we have a ranch to develop," Hannah said proudly.

We high-fived, and everyone hugged before climbing into their cars.

From what I had seen, Hannah was a sweet and gentle woman. Me? No way. I was more of a tell-it-like-it-is and get on with the business at hand type of person. I hoped we would continue to get along despite our differences. The next few months could be stressful with so much work to do on the ranch project and, of course, planning our weddings.

"Montana or bust," I exclaimed as I drove Alice, Clint, and Shadow in our Suburban. Troy followed in his truck with Billy at his side and his horse Gunner in the trailer. The first stop for us was the airport near Casper. The senior members of the McAllister family would fly home.

Next in line was Hannah driving the Jeep with a box on the back seat containing the cat and her two kittens. Oatie and the pup, Little Charlie, rode with Trace in his truck. He had two horses in his trailer: his gelding, Black-jack, and his dad's mare, Milagro – Millie for short. They'd take a slight detour to drop off Clint's horse near Golden, Colorado.

We'd traveled a mere five minutes on the rough dirt road when we heard loud popping noises. Was it an explosion? Gunshots? Falling trees? I quickly wondered. I slammed on my brakes and, looking in my rearview mirror, saw that everyone had stopped. Good, no rear end collisions today.

Troy and Trace were already out and on their feet staring at rising dark puffs of smoke. That's not good. The H-I Double M Ranch had the only buildings within miles. Sure, the smoke could be a careless camper or an old, lightning strike flare up, but those things would not sound like an explosion. And only a fool would camp in this area in the dead of winter. A freaky Mother Nature phenomenon or an act of God seemed more logical to me.

"Kitchi!" Hannah shouted. "We've got to go back and check on him."

I knew Hannah was right. Was this the trouble Kitchi had hinted at earlier? With no way to move Clint quickly or safely, he and Alice would stay behind with Billy and Shadow. I grabbed the gun Troy kept under the Suburban's front seat and placed it in Clint's hand. "Just in case trouble stops by," I said, attempting a worry-free tone. We all piled into the Jeep, Hannah put it in four-wheel drive and managed to turn the vehicle around kicking up gravel, dirt, and remnants of an earlier snowfall. We sped off to check on Kitchi, the large cabin, and the small barn.

It was true that all the troublemakers who had showed

up in our lives the past few months were either dead or in jail. So where was the trouble coming from this time?

I was hoping for a simple mistake committed by Mother Nature.

Hannah

IVY SAT in the front seat with me. Trace and Troy crowded into the back with the box of cats. No time to buckle up. Seeing the smoke spiraling up toward the blue sky encouraged me to step heavily on the gas peddle. I had to admit, I was getting pretty good at driving fast on rough dirt roads.

"Hold onto the cats, Trace. The worst bumps and ruts are still ahead of us," I said firmly, loudly as my hands nearly strangled the steering wheel.

The roof of the cabin came into view first. "I don't think the smoke is coming from the cabin," Troy said, leaning his head out the open window for a better look. His timing couldn't have been worse. The Jeep swerved, dipping down into a deep rut in the road and everyone's heads hit the ceiling. The cats went flying, a shrill, roller-coaster-ride sound was uttered by three adults. Troy's forehead met with the metal surrounding the space created by the open window. His utterance was pure pain.

Ivy, in spite of the speed and the bumps, was on her knees looking back at Troy. "Are you okay?" she asked. "You're going to need some ice on that fast growing goose egg."

I slowed down but only a little. We'd reach the cabin and the barn with in a minute or two and we didn't need any additional problems to pop up. Still, time was of the essence. Troy held his head in his hands. Trace had rounded up the cats who seemed happy to be back in their box, and now he stared out the front window poised and ready for whatever we'd face next.

"That's a lot of smoke coming from the barn." I spoke the obvious. We'd all underestimated the amount of the swirling gray smoke because a breeze had taken it in a different direction toward the largest grove of trees west of the barn. Screeching to a stop inches from the steps leading to the cabin's front door, we all piled out.

Trace and Troy dashed toward the smoking barn, Ivy dug through one of my coolers for an ice pack, and I made sure the cats were safely in the Jeep with the windows cracked just a little.

Ivy and I headed to the barn calling out to Kitchi with every step. No reply ever came and I prayed he wasn't in the burning building. We could see flames flickering through the cracks in the old wooden walls.

"Stand back," Trace shouted. "We're going in but as

soon as we open the doors, the additional oxygen might cause a major flare up."

"Shouldn't we call for help?" I shouted back not wanting anyone to get hurt. We weren't firefighters. We didn't even have a hose hooked up.

"There's no help close enough. We've got to handle it ourselves." Trace was a strong independent man. Still, I'd come to know him well and detected stress and worry in his voice.

"Troy, I've got an ice pack for you. That lump on your head is growing."

"Later, babe. We've got a fire to extinguish first. If we don't hurry, there will nothing left.

We stood back, though not very far, feeling powerless and wishing there was something we could do to help. The men reached for the latches on the double doors, and they both shook their heads. Were the doors too hot to handle? Probably. Their hands had no gloves, but their feet had boots. And, oh, boy, did they use them. It was as if they were stunt men in a movie. Not that the doors opencd but the men were able to kick through the old wooden doors.

"We're in luck. Looks like the fire started on the far side of barn and now its merely flickering. And, with the floor being just dirt, we can do this. So come in if you want to, ladies. We're going put the darn fire completely out."

Immediately, Ivy and I stepped over the broken threshold. We reached for the rake and shovel that were propped against the wall near the newly kicked-in entryway when . . . whoosh! Smoke swirled filling the space around us. Ivy made it out first. Trace grabbed me around my waist and we were out seconds later. Troy brought up the rear. Though coughing and a bit shaken, we'd all made it outside to breathable air unharmed. Though slower than expected, the influx of oxygen had sparked new life in the glowing embers as Trace had mentioned earlier, and almost did us in. Yes, we were very lucky.

"That was a close one. Too close. So what now?" I knew that a guardian angel must have been watching over us, and I prayed that the worst might have passed. All I desired was a take-two and to be homeward bound.

"As long as the wind doesn't pick up suddenly, I think we're good to go back in. Please wait outside, ladies. Trace and I are going to be raking and shoveling dirt on anything that is still smoldering or glowing."

"At least wait a few minutes to catch your breath." I insisted on that, and, at the same time, I loved that our guys projected an aura of *all is well* on our behalf.

"Hannah, your face has some soot on it."

I looked at Ivy, then at Trace and Troy. We'd all been baptized with a bit of the black dust. "I'll go get some wet wipes from my Jeep. Be right back."

I'd just made it to the car when the grave danger we'd all faced struck me. Yes, it felt like an actual blow. I leaned against the door for support as exhaustion swept over me and I told myself to take slow, deep breaths. I could get through this. I'd been through much worse in the past.

Meowing. I heard meowing. Of course, the cats were in the Jeep, and their calling to me brought me back to a much-needed alertness.

I wiped my face clean while I could see my reflection on the window and hurried back to the others with the wet wipes in hand.

"Thanks, Hannah. So glad you had these in your Jeep," Ivy said as she removed the soot from her face.

"Hey, I think we're done," Trace said as he walked out of the barn.

"Yeah, we did it. Although let's stick around for a while to make sure a stray spark doesn't reignite."

We stood together just beyond the charred barn needing to process the event as we watched and waited. We also paced in place. My term for shifting one's weight from one foot to the other. For me, the movement had a double purpose: to keep warm and shake off the remnants of fear or worry.

"Could this be a case of spontaneous combustion?" Ivy asked.

"I suppose so, but I'm pretty sure someone started this fire," I said, "though not necessarily with the intention of burning down the barn."

"What's that supposed to mean?" All eyes were on me waiting for an answer.

My nose was trying to tell me something. "There was a new scent lingering between the barn and the cabin that had not been there earlier."

"How do you know that?" Troy asked.

Trace knew the answer. "My Hannah has an incredible sense of smell. Even better than Oatie's sometimes."

"I smelled something similar to an accelerant."

Ivy's booted foot began to tap nervously. "Then why didn't this old place burn to the ground?"

"I don't think the accelerant made it to the barn. The scent was primarily half way between the two structures. Possibly, it was dropped or spilled."

"Maybe the arsonist got cold feet, or figured someone was still on the property and gave up the plan before the real pyrotechnics got going," Trace said. "If that was his intention."

"Or hers," I added.

Trace's comment was perfectly logical. Still, I'd feel much better if I knew where Kitchi was. I was sure Ivy felt the same. Our ranch project work list just got longer. At least the exterior walls and roof, though covered in soot, were still standing. I assumed that was one thing we could be thankful for.

We all walked around the barn's exterior several times looking for clues to who might have been there, and we also called Kitchi's name over and over. No reply came, but on the way back to the Jeep I saw that his truck and horse trailer was still parked behind the cabin. I didn't see the horse, though. We gathered in front of the cabin for one more discussion before heading out.

Ivy's foot no longer tapped. "I think I know approximately where he is."

"Okay. Spill those beans, Ivy," Troy said. "We need to find him."

"He's probably off in the trees doing his daily cardio and wild workout. He uses the woods, the outdoors, as a gym. He told me all about that the day I briefly lost Shadow."

"I think I knew that, but why would he take his horse?" Troy asked, staring straight ahead.

"My thoughts exactly, but don't we need to check on Clint, Alice, and Billy? I'm sure they're worried and if your parents miss their plane we'll have another situation on our hands."

Troy insisted that he take on the task. "I'll let them know what's happened and that we will get them to airport in time to catch their plane."

"All right. The keys are in Jeep," I said. "Do you mind bringing Billy and the rest of the pets back with you? I think we may need to be here for a while and I don't want to worry about them too."

"I'll be back in less than ten minutes with a Jeep full of cats and dogs and my adorable little boy."

Seconds after Troy drove off, Kitchi came running up huffing and puffing. "I took an extra long run today. Got too far from home." He noticed the open barn doors and looked at Ivy, Trace, and me. "Why are you back? What's going on?"

"Didn't you hear the snapping, popping noises or smell the smoke?" Ivy asked.

"No. I'd gone too far, too fast, over several ridges."

Relieved to know that he was all right, Ivy informed him that we had some trouble in the old barn and we took him for a quick look. He said nothing, but shook his head.

Minutes later, we were all standing in front of the cabin. I felt something didn't add up. "Where is your horse?" I asked Kitchi. No answer came. He just took off running.

Ivy shook her head and shrugged. "That is so like Kitchi. It takes a while to get used his way of moving through life. Trust me, Hannah, he's brilliant and wise."

"If you say so. Let's go make sure all's well inside the main cabin while we wait for Troy to get back," I suggested, hoping Kitchi and his horse would be back by then too.

As I slipped the new key that Clint had given me into the lock, I spotted a folded piece of paper stuck between the door and the jamb.

"Looks like our visitor left us a note. An apology for setting a fire in our barn, perhaps?"

My sarcasm was meant to instill levity; however, it failed. I handed the note to Trace and prepared to study his reaction as his eyes scanned the words. Those eyes glazed over. A blank look was all I saw. So I knew the words were troublesome and added to his concern.

"The note seems to be from—"

"I hear a car," Ivy shouted with excessive enthusiasm and extremely poor timing. "It's headed this way." She kept her eyes on the dirt road until the vehicle came into view. "It's Troy. Thank God."

Troy parked my Jeep a few feet from where the three of us stood waiting and got out. Smiling, he let Oatie, Little Charlie, and Shadow out knowing they would stay close to their humans. The cats remained in the Jeep.

"Where's Billy? I thought you were bringing him back."

"Well, yes. That was the plan, but plans do change."

"I'm surprised he didn't beg to come back with you," Ivy said looking up into Troy's eyes.

Troy's face seemed to brighten with amusement, and he said, "Oh, he begged."

"And you wouldn't let him come?" Ivy asked with a frown on her face.

"He begged to stay with Grandma and Grandpa. Said he'd keep them safe."

"Ah. That's our boy," she replied.

I could not stand the suspense. Not even for one more second. "Read the note, Trace. Read it out loud."

"A note? From who?" Troy looked surprised.

"Here's what it says: *Beware! You McAllisters won't get away with it. You've been warned.*"

Those disturbing words seemed to take everyone's breath away. We'd all had our fair share of danger over the past few months – more than most people have in a lifetime. Enough! We didn't need anymore. Ever!

"Get away with what?" Ivy asked, her eyes squinting.

"Yeah. What does that mean?" Troy wanted to know too.

"I have no idea. This makes no sense," Trace added. "Especially here in Wyoming."

"I guess we can't pin this on Mother Nature. But how did the note writer even get here?" I asked. "No way could he or she have gotten around our caravan of cars and trucks, and no other road leads to our undeveloped old ranch."

"We can't leave Billy in the Suburban much longer," Troy stated. "And I don't want Mom and Dad to miss their plane." He was right. We needed to hurry.

"Agreed!" Ivy said. "I don't know about you, but I'm getting cold. While we're still together, let's go inside for a three-minute, stand-up conversation to create a mental list of any McAllister haters that we know of."

No one objected. A three-minute delay to our departure wouldn't make much of a difference. Troy stationed himself at the front window watching the pets who were hanging out on the porch. I'm certain he was keeping an eye out for far more than that.

Trace and I came up with a few names. The first two were Rick, my ex-friend who was supposed to share The Lucky Seven with me, and his twin brother, Rudy. Either one or both of them together wanted to steal the money I'd recently won in the lottery. Then there was the jealous bad girl, Callie, who wanted to steal Trace from me.

Troy didn't mention any names but he said, "We just had a Chicago gangster and his goons try to steal my fictitious treasure and kill us all in the process." Someday, I will ask Ivy to tell me more about that.

So many thoughts ran through my head. It seemed all but the bad girl (though she had been an accomplice) were willing to kill. Their motive? Money. Lots of money. But those men could not be involved in this. Not way out here. Besides, they were dead or in prison. No. This was merely a threat to scare us; after all, the note-writer had demanded nothing, although that fact was troublesome too.

"Shouldn't we call the police?" Ivy asked.

"Nope," Trace answered. "The closest law enforcement is in Casper. They'd take forever to get here, if they'd come at all. But you've given me an idea, Ivy. We could contact the property manager."

"You know," Troy began, "Dad is the only one that might have some answers. Maybe the threat is tied to this property somehow. That's the only thing that would make any sense. He could check with the property manager too."

"We must get this figured out and the villain destroyed before Hannah and I can move forward with our ranch project. So, time is of the essence."

My creative juices didn't flow when I had to keep on the lookout for bad guys. I completely agreed with Ivy's urgency.

Troy looked at both of us. "Ladies, you're not coming back here until this mystery is solved or it just goes away… and stays away. Come on, Ivy, let's get Mom and Dad to the airport. On the way back we'll get Billy a hamburger and fries."

Back outside on the patio, we waved at the departing duo as they took off in my Jeep. Walking all the way to where the Suburban was parked would take too long. Troy and Ivy would drive the SUV and all its occupants to the airport. That was the plan. And time was still of the essence, especially for Clint and Alice. If they missed their plane, it could be a day or two before another flight would depart from the small airport near Casper. For now, the only vehicle by the cabin was Kitchi's truck. But he wasn't here and neither were the keys.

A new sound coming from the open field just north of the cabin caught our attention. "Sounds like snow crunching under running feet to me." I hoped it was Kitchi.

"Sure does. We'll, know for sure in—"

"Kitchi! We're so glad you got back before we headed out for the second time. The way things have been going around here, your brief absence made me worry again," I said. "Take a moment to catch your breath. How about some coffee?"

"Sure."

We sat at the kitchen table silently sipping the freshly made coffee.

Both Trace and Kitchi were men of few words. This I knew. Though Kitchi's lack of conversation was more extreme. So I was surprised when he spoke first.

"I take it there is another problem."

"Yeah, we've had more trouble. Would you mind checking on the horses and the vehicles parked about half way to the paved road? I'd feel much better if I knew all was well. Troy and Ivy are rushing to get Clint and Alice to the airport with no time to spare."

"No problem. I will look for my horse on the way." He stood and headed for the front door. We watched as he took off running.

"I thought you might drive your truck," I called after him. He never turned around; he just waved and kept on going. Trying to figure that man out was a waste of energy.

Trace and I put the dogs inside so we could scout around the area behind and to the south of the cabin undisturbed and look for clues. We hadn't ventured in that direction before. Part of me wanted to bring Oatie. He was such a brilliant cattle dog. I hoped we wouldn't regret leaving him behind.

Except for the dirt road where our numerous vehicles

had packed down and worn away the snow, the rest of the area was still covered with six to twelve inches of the white stuff. At first, close to the cabin, we walked in snow likely disturbed by our pets and Billy dashing about. But then Trace and I noticed an unusual path veering off, heading away from cabin. No dog or little boy boot prints went that way. That path looked as if a fallen branch had carved it, so we followed the odd trail. It curved and zigzagged.

I thought about heading back to the cabin when the path became a trail of footprints. Two pair of prints coming and going.

"Do you think we should we wait for Troy and Ivy, you know, for back up?" I assumed these two people were the ones responsible for delivering the threatening note and starting a fire in the barn.

"I've got my gun, so let's go a little further, darlin'. However, my feet are getting darn cold in these cowboy boots."

I think he hoped I would laugh at his words. I didn't. My feet were darn cold too, and I was wearing fur lined snow boots.

Trace stopped walking and talking and wrapped me in his arms. Even through our winter clothing, I felt his warmth, his love. He kissed my forehead before saying into my ear, "No one knows the McAllisters in this remote area of Wyoming. Dad hasn't been here in 40 years and then only for a short while."

"True, but I know I heard someone mention a property manager. He could be our villain with an accomplice. He definitely knows about this property. Or maybe this is a case of mistaken identity."

"But, Hannah, the threat is for the McAllisters. That's us. I hope Dad has some answers. We need to know what we're up against."

"I agree. It's hard to fight the unknown."

"One thing is for sure. We'll build our arsenals, and do some target practice as soon as we get back to Colorado."

Trace's mention of shooting guns came as a surprise to me. I knew I needed to practice shooting and become familiar with how guns operate. I just hated the thought of needing to possess that talent.

To lighten the darkening mood, I said, "Sounds like we're preparing for a zombie apocalypse."

My joke fell flat. My skills at kidding around needed work, or possibly my timing was off today. We decided to keep walking and follow the footprints a bit farther. After walking a while, we stopped abruptly and stared at the ground ahead. Red splashes stood out on the glistening, whiteness of the snow. Dots of red were on a few of the trees too.

I gasped. "Blood?" I looked at Trace not wanting that to be his answer.

Trace touched the redness with his finger. "Still wet," he said giving it a sniff. "Paint. It's just paint, but why would someone bring paint to the property?"

I felt better . . . but only a little.

"We have to stop this, whatever *this* is."

Hearing the sound of a vehicle – I prayed it was the Suburban with Troy, Ivy, and Billy – we hurried back to the cabin to share what we'd discovered and, hopefully, learn that Clint was able to fill in a few of our blanks.

CHAPTER TWO

IVY

I leaped from the SUV with a large white paper bag filled with cheeseburgers. Billy held the bag with the french fries. "Let's eat," he said excitedly. We all headed to the kitchen.

Hannah and Trace seemed glad to see us with the food, and although we had passed out all the burgers and fries, no one had taken a bite yet.

"Tell them what we learned, Troy," I said.

"Not a damn thing. Dad has no idea what this threat is all about. He did add that once they were settled back in their condo in Golden, he'd search for any and all paperwork associated with this property."

"I'll look around The Big Mack, too, for evidence of that old transaction making Dad the owner."

Billy snuggled up to me and asked, "Can I give the dogs their special treats now?"

"Shadow has already had hers, so you better ask the dogs' mommy if it's okay with her."

"Uh, Aunt Hannah, can Oatie and Little Charlie have a burger? I got one for each and they are plain, plain, plain, so it shouldn't upset their tummies."

"Let me see . . . hmm. Yes! It's a definite yes, since you were so conscientious about the dogs' well-being," Hannah said.

The conversation circled back to the note and the fire.

"I've heard enough for today," Trace said impatiently. "We need to get home to keep our ranches and animals safe."

"I agree. Because someone, somewhere knows way too much about us," Hannah said with a touch of anger.

We were all angry and losing tolerance for those who wished to do us harm. Memories of the no-gooders, the killers, the thieves, and the kidnappers of our not-so-distant-past remained raw, influencing our thinking, even our emotions.

"I'm anxious to get our crew back to Montana," I said. "And I bet the horses are tired of being confined to the horse trailers."

"Yeah, probably," Troy said as he scratched his head. "Trace, did you give the horses some extra oats?"

"Nope. Might have been Kitchi. I did ask him to check on the horses. I think he ran the entire way from here, but he might have seen the bags of oats in the trailers and given them some. Or possibly the horses hadn't eaten what we'd given earlier."

"Huh. There was no sign of him there or on the road between here and there. Where could he be?" Troy tended to be protective of his right-hand man. Actually, that worked both ways.

I wasn't too worried. Kitchi was his own man with his own way of dealing with life, death, nature . . . always taking everything in stride and showing no outward signs of stress or worry. Sometimes, I wished I could be more like him.

"So what did you guys do while we were gone?" I teased, and took it upon myself to be the one to lighten the mood.

Trace began telling the story of their time alone. Hannah added a detail now and then. After hearing the account of the odd snowy path, the footprints, and the blood-red paint, I hoped Kitchi turned up before we attempted to head home again.

Hannah put her hand up like a student asking to be called on except she didn't wait for that to happen.

"Before we go our separate ways could we spend just a few more minutes to revisit the list of the people we've crossed paths with," she said. "Maybe we missed something."

Darrell and Luke's names popped up in the conversation right away. I couldn't believe we'd forgotten about them, but then Clint was their victim, not any of us. Not directly anyway.

"I'll contact the deputies who tried to pin Clint's injuries on Trace and I just a few weeks ago," Troy said. "They would know if and where Darrell and Luke were incarcerated."

Knowing for sure, we could cross them off our current list of suspects, at least for what had happened here.

Troy paced across the living room shaking his head. "They could still be responsible for harassing us by enlisting a friend or relative. We know they are ruthless, dim-witted men, and without a doubt, they're pissed off at the McAllisters."

A quick hush fell over the room, and we seemed to be wrapped up in an unusual stillness. Silence loomed, making my ears ring from the absence of noise.

My EMT and paramedic experience warned me that Hannah's sudden, rapid breathing could soon become full-on hyperventilation. I quickly brought her a glass of water from the kitchen and insisted she drink some.

"Thanks, Ivy. I think the stress of today got to me."

"That's understandable. We're all feeling a bit keyed up."

Hannah, still sounding a little breathless, managed to squeak out some important words.

"The men's modus operandi was to write notes. Our vandals here left a note too. So far, Darrell and Luke's connection is the only thing that makes a little sense."

Everyone's eyes grew wide with excitement at the promise of an answer. Affirmative nods suggested agreement. The prospect of solving a small part of this mystery jarred my memory. "Troy, didn't you set up your game camera on the side of the cabin last week?"

"Sure did." We all ran outside and I do mean all. Billy and the dogs came too. None of us wore jackets; none of us felt the cold. We were on a mission.

The only laptop with us was packed away, so we were limited to checking the photos—if there were any—right there on the camera.

"There's a lot of photos here but most look the same. Just the landscape. Oh, wait. There's a bird." I hadn't meant to be humorous, though my words got a laugh. There really was a photo of a bird.

Our clue-hunting trail grew colder than the air around us as we stared at the photos snapped by the game camera.

We'd almost given up when Trace said, "Wait. I think I see the outline of two people."

Yes, Trace was right but viewing the photos on the camera's tiny screen made everything look dark and blurry. Not much help.

Troy had been quiet for a while as we all stared at the camera, but now he spoke. "Despite the poor quality of the photos, we can be pretty sure that two people walked here to the cabin, wrote a note, and started a small fire. The time stamp on each photo proved they were here shortly after our caravan pulled out this morning."

Hannah added, "And after Trace and I saw their path and the prints in the snow, we knew they travelled on foot quite a distance across fields and around small crops of trees. Their attempt to cover that up, failed."

"They probably left in a hurry once they noticed Kitchi's truck and horse trailer." I agreed with Trace's assessment. "Speaking of Kitchi, I wonder if he could still be looking for his horse? And the bigger question in my mind? Should we be looking for him?"

"Come on, babe. We can't wait for Kitchi. We need to get going."

With heavy hearts we went back inside to grab our coats and make sure we hadn't forgotten anything. Trace locked up and we all walked slowly toward the Suburban and climbed in. I drove, Troy had Billy and the coyote on his lap. Hannah sat in the back with Trace and the remaining pets. It was cozy to say the least. It was fortunate that the drive to the other vehicles was a short one.

Still, everything about today felt wrong from the moment Kitchi and I spoke in the living room. What had he said? Oh, yeah, *so far, everything is all right*.

We'd driven less than 100 feet when Billy pointed out the window and shouted, "Look, Mom. I see them."

At first, I was thrilled to see Kitchi and his horse coming out of the trees. As they got a little closer, I knew there was a problem. The horse moved very slowly with her head hanging down. I stopped the SUV. Hannah and I got out and hurried to meet them.

"What happened?" Hannah asked. "Is she injured?"

"She's not well."

That much we'd figured out ourselves. Often, Kitchi's comments lacked details, which was extremely frustrating.

"Would you like me to call a vet?" Ivy asked before knowing if that was even possible.

"No."

"Then what do you want to do for her right now?"

"Nothing," the man said stoically. "The horse and I will walk together, though I fear she may be unsavable."

Hannah and I had an immediate, though brief, conversation right then and there and made a plan for the horse. Nothing? We could not do *nothing*, and Kitchi seemed to be in some kind of trance. So, we led the horse slowly to her trailer.

"What is your horse's name, Kitchi?" Hannah asked. When no answer came, she asked again. "Your horse must have a name. What do you call her?"

He didn't look up but said, "Clover. Chloe for short."

Hannah walked in front of Kitchi's horse, Chloe, and the horse followed her.

I'd heard rumors about Hannah's special powers when it came to communicating with animals. Perhaps, they were true. I walked alongside the horse gently patting its withers, and Kitchi took up the rear. It was a short walk, so even moving slowly, it didn't take long.

We removed the center rail making this two-horse trailer wide enough for the horse to lie down comfortably if she wanted to. Hannah insisted that Trace help her cover the trailer's floor with hay and straw. We offered Chloe some water before loading her in. Troy was able to ease her into a lying-down position. The horse went down willingly as if that was what she wanted to do.

Troy nudged me. "Now, we really need to get going."

I hated to leave Kitchi and Chloe, but we'd done all that we could for now.

"Please bring her back to Montana. I will take full responsibility for her until she's well – as long as she's not suffering."

Kitchi's reply was merely a nod.

CHAPTER THREE

HANNAH

I was doing my best to adjust to life back at The Lucky Seven Ranch after spending nearly four weeks in Wyoming. Trace and I were not together all of that time, though. He and Troy had been out defying death in wild Wyoming amid blizzard conditions. All Ivy and I knew was that they were determined to arrive at the designated assembly point, where Clint's Challenge would finally end. And each man wanted to be first so he could win some sort of untold award their dad had dangled in front of them like a carrot. Waiting, not knowing if they were safe, was tough. I shuddered as I thought back on those days, those feelings of wondering if they were even alive.

Later, after the men returned, Trace had stayed in Casper to travel between the hospital and the vet's office where Oatie had surgery from the injury he acquired searching for Clint with Trace and Troy. Clint needed time in the hospital to recover from his own injuries. What was the man thinking assigning himself a similar Wyoming winter challenge?

Now, life here was so calm, so dream-like that I often felt bewildered and sleepy. I gave myself three days to snap out of this do-nothing funk. I hadn't even called Ivy, which I felt bad about, but then she hadn't called me either.

Trace, the love of my life, stayed by my side the first two days we were home. We held hands and walked to the lower pasture to check on my four cows: Buttercup, Good & Plenty, Bubbles, and Betty. I liked to think that the cows understood their names. A fantasy, I know. Still, every time I said the name Betty she looked up, and it made me laugh. We put halters and lead ropes on my two horses, Lewissa and Clark, and took them for walks. I didn't feel up to riding yet.

Now, day three had arrived. What would I do with it?

"Hannah, darlin', I need to check in with Rosa and Harry at The Big Mack today," Trace whispered into my ear. He wrapped his arms around me as I stood at the kitchen sink. "Do you want come with me?"

Did I? Part of me did. I wasn't ready for Trace to let go of me, not even for a minute, let alone for a day. I loved his touch, his scent, his warmth. But I understood that his main ranch needed him too. He'd never been away this long before.

"Uh, Hannah. Are you just going let the water keep running?"

"No, of course not."

What is the matter with me? The sink was about to overflow. Even with Trace's announcement, some water spilled onto the floor due to my slow reaction time. I have become one with the phrase *dazed and confused*. How could one poorly written note left at the Wyoming cabin hundreds of miles from here bother me so much? I was home now, safe and sound.

"Thank you, but I think I'll pass on your offer today. Right after I mop up the wet floor, I'm going to spend some one-on-one time with Lewissa; she's always a good listener and she's capable of making me laugh."

We kissed on the lips. The first kiss was short and sweet. The second one – long and passionate. In need of air, we each stepped back. The intense gaze from his eyes to mine created an invisible lifeline still holding us together.

"I'm going to leave Oatie and Little Charlie here if that's okay with you."

Both dogs sat just a few feet from us smiling and tilting their heads as if waiting for my answer. My answer would always be yes! With the horses and the dogs nearby, I felt secure. Trace knew that.

"I'll keep my cell phone and my SAT phone with me. Call anytime. Relax, darlin', and get some rest because when I get back, we have work to do."

I was curious. What did he mean by that? He gave no clues; not even his usual grin. The only work I needed to do was to mop the floor by my feet, my wet feet. I should have put shoes on this morning, warm shoes.

Well, they are on now. Glancing out the kitchen window, I saw Lewissa and Clark standing side by side looking toward the house. I think they missed me as much as I missed them. I grabbed a carrot for my mare and an apple for Clark, the gelding. They deserved an extra treat on this chilly January morning.

"Hello, Lewissa. How's my girl?" The mare nuzzled my neck with her velvety nose. "I missed you too." Then I gave her the carrot. Clark took his apple gently and began chewing. I loved these horses so much. I'd never been near a horse until I left Phoenix and ended up here. "I don't want to be so far away from the two of you and The Lucky Seven ever again."

Right then, my eyes glazed over as I stared blankly down our long gravel driveway. The reality of the ranch project hit me. I'd be making many trips back to Wyoming if Ivy and I moved forward and developed the property Clint had awarded us. Lewissa must have sensed my inattention. When I looked up, she and Clark were playfully chasing each other around the paddock, taking me from my worrisome thoughts, and making me smile.

Jostled by the sudden sound of my phone ringing, I was diverted from watching my beloved animals once again. So much for relaxing with my horses.

"Hello?"

"Hi, Hannah. It's Ivy. What's going on down there in Colorado?"

I took a deep breath and prepared to sound confident, energetic, and ready to take on the world or at least our ranch project should that topic come up.

"Hi, Ivy. Not much. We spent the past two days walking around The Lucky Seven with the animals. Trace headed over to the main ranch today after telling me to get some rest. That's about it. How about you?"

"They say there's no rest for the wicked, so I must be really wicked."

"You don't sound tired. A little wired maybe, but not tired."

"Kitchi stayed away longer than we expected. Fortunately, no guests visit the ranch in mid-winter, but several of the wranglers and Saige, the registrar and mixologist, were there all expecting Kitchi to prepare three meals a day for them. That's what they were used to."

"So, what happened?"

"Apparently, they fended for themselves and left quite a mess. Normally, Troy doesn't tolerate any type of disarray, but he felt awful that he hadn't given any thought to the consequences of Kitchi's absence. In his defense, he didn't know Kitchi was going to leave the ranch. It was a total surprise when he arrived at the Wyoming cabin on Christmas Eve."

"Yes, this past Christmas was packed with unusual events, surprises, and emotions."

"That's one way of describing those few weeks, Hannah. Anyway, the second we got back, we became the cooks, the dishwashers, and the supply purchasers. I didn't have time to be tired or to do too much thinking. Kitchi showed up last night with his living, upright horse in tow, but stated that she was not out of the woods yet. Chloe still had health issues. Apparently, that was a story for another day, but I restated my offer to help with his horse."

"I think the four of us should get together in the very near future . . . maybe on a Zoom call," I suggested.

Ivy and I decided to put off discussing the ranch project for a few more days. Neither of us had taken the time to think about it. But now that we were both home and away from those weeks of worrying about the survival of our men, we chose to chat about our recent near-death pasts and the fears that lingered among those memories.

"I may know a bit more about your situation since Trace flew to Montana for a short visit," Ivy said. "He saved our lives, you know, and he mentioned that you were the reason he was there. So, thank you, Hannah. If Trace hadn't shown up when he did, there'd be no ranch project, no wedding, no us."

"You're welcome. When I heard that Trace had an older brother and they hadn't seen each other in years, I insisted he go for a visit." Now that I recalled that conversation, I couldn't suppress a laugh.

"What's so funny, Hannah?"

"I wanted to see photos of The Lonely Horse Ranch and Troy. So I asked Trace to 'shoot everything' while he was there. I had no idea the 'shooting' would be gunfire."

"Yeah, that part of our deadly affair came after the kidnapping, the plane crash, and the treacherous search and rescue. Troy told me you were kidnapped also."

"I was, right from the front porch at The Lucky Seven. The man was my friend Rick's twin brother, Rudy . . . we think. Anyway, he heard I was a lucky lottery winner. He'd stop at nothing to get his hands on my money. He kidnapped me and tried to kill me twice. He came close to killing Trace too. We think he killed his own brother. He was a very bad man, but he's dead and gone now. We're almost certain of that."

"Thank God."

"Yes, for sure, but I still have nightmares about Rudy and all the horrible things he did."

It seemed that all those who'd wished us harm were gone for good. That's why the fire and the note at the cabin made no sense at all. Was it an unrelated event we needn't worry about?

Ivy and I were amazed at our parallel lives. We had so much in common. We were each in love with a ranch-owning McAllister man; we experienced terrifying, deadly situations that involved them; and we received great comfort from our animals too.

"What filled your time before hooking up with Troy?" I asked.

"I was an EMT and a paramedic. That was a tough, exhausting job. My knowledge of fixing sick or broken bodies has come in handy quite a lot since I met Troy. When I wasn't working, I was at the gym building my strength or getting some much needed sleep. Now, I just want to be Troy's wife, Billy's mom, and write a novel in my spare time."

"Spare time, huh? I don't foresee much of that in our

future if we want to make any headway with our ranch project."

"We'll be so organized, we will do it all and then some," Ivy said.

"Keep telling me that because I'd rather not give up drawing, painting, and growing things."

"Growing things? Like what?"

"Food, herbs, and anything I can use for making essential oils."

"Wow! I'm impressed. Maybe our ranch should be a spa retreat or a glam-camping dude ranch," Ivy said with a chuckle. "Just kidding."

"We haven't even mentioned our upcoming weddings." I wished for a take-two, a do-over. My statement reflected a real concern, but I hadn't meant to sound so darn whiney.

"You're right, but we will. And I have a good idea." Ivy's voice dropped to a whisper. "Troy just walked in. I'll call you tomorrow."

Ivy

THE MINUTE KITCHI had returned to The Lonely Horse Ranch, he'd settled his horse in one of the well-insulated stalls and asked me to walk her as often as possible.

47

"Had some colic and needs to keep walking."

"Sure, Kitchi. I'm happy to help your horse," I said. "Would it be all right if Billy sat on Chloe's back when I do walk her?"

"Yes."

He said nothing more, then acted as if he'd never been gone or returned from Wyoming days later than we expected. I watched him head toward the ranch's kitchen seeming anxious to get back to his usual work and routines.

I continued tending to Chloe as I'd promised, checking on her and walking her morning, noon, and night. The slow walking seemed to be making a difference, and I sensed there was hope for the horse.

But since his return from our Wyoming adventure, Kitchi seemed to be living inside of his head, rarely looking up. I didn't understand his actions because he was never part of the danger. Was he still worried about Chloe? Or had something else occupied his thoughts? I'd give him some space, though not for very long.

My mid-day walk with Billy and Chloe was nearly over. Just as well because the temperature was dropping rapidly. "Look, Mom. I'm smoking," Billy said blowing puffs of air from his mouth.

"Yep. Me, too. So is the horse."

"Can we stop by Miss Saige's office? I can see it from

here."

I put on a thinking-hard expression. "I suppose so, but she's working, you know. We can't take up too much of her time."

"Everybody's working. Dad, Mr. Kitchi, and the wranglers are all busy doing important work. Everybody but me." Billy's lower lip might have hit the ground if he hadn't been sitting on a horse. "I want to work too. Even you work, Mom."

"What is my job?" I asked, but did I want his answer? He was taking too long to come up with one.

"I saw you wash clothes a few times."

I suppose that was one of those *out of the mouths of babes* moments. "Let's go say hi to Saige."

Saige must have seen us coming because she stood in the doorway smiling as we arrived. "Look at you up on that big horse. You're becoming quite the cowboy, Billy."

"Yes, ma'am. But today, I'm looking for a job."

Saige and I made eye contact and shrugged. Silence prevailed for a few seconds, the only sound came from Chloe. Billy laughed. "She likes to do that with her lips. I can do it too." And sure enough, he could.

I wondered if there was a name for that sound. I'd ask Troy tonight. "Bye, Saige, we'll see you—"

"Do you still want a job, Billy?"

The boy, now wide-eyed, nodded. "Yes!"

"Wonderful. You're hired, if it's okay with Ivy."

"Can I, Mom?"

"Uh, sure." What in the world did she have in mind?

"Great." Saige moved closer, reached up, and lifted Billy down from the horse. "See you in about an hour."

"Okay, if you're sure that's all right with you," I said, walking away with the riderless horse. The clip-clopping sound of Chloe's hooves was pleasant and relaxing. That's when an idea popped into my head. Troy's office was my next stop.

I tossed the horse's long lead rope over the wooden railing outside of the lodge and let myself in. From the main door, I could see Troy sitting at his desk. He must have been deep in thought because he didn't notice my entrance or my presence until I placed my hands on his shoulders.

"This is a pleasant surprise. I thought you were walking Kitchi's horse with Billy."

"I was, but then Billy got a job and I got an idea."

He closed the ledger he'd been reading, swiveled his chair around, and pulled me onto his lap. "That sounds interesting. Tell me all about it."

"Well, we stopped by to see Saige for just a minute, and our little guy told her he was looking for a job. She offered one, and he took it. I won't know the details of his work until I pick him up in an hour."

"And your idea?"

"It's been an odd season so far with our absence and Kitchi's time away too. Your staff is so loyal, and they rarely complain so, I'd like to do something special for all the employees that stayed on for the winter."

"Okay. What do you have in mind?" he asked.

"Nothing too difficult, though I will ask Kitchi to help me."

"I take it this involves food, the kitchen, and the dining hall."

"You got two out of three."

He lifted my chin and stared into my eyes, giving me one of his I'm-not-going-to-play-twenty-questions looks. I stood up, leaned against his desk, and began to explain. "I'd like all of us, every staff member that is here, to have a little winter celebration – just togetherness, all around one table, enjoying a good meal. And I'd like to set it up in the saloon not the dining hall. I walked through there yesterday to see how the clean-up and final stages of the mini remodel turned out. Looked better than ever," I said with a wink. "And I couldn't find a single bullet hole or splatter of blood. So, what do you think?"

"Sure. Go for it, as long as you can get Kitchi on board."

I bent down and nibbled Troy's ear, then whispered, "I'm on it!"

"Of that, I have no doubt."

He walked me to the door of his private office, which I had left open when I entered. To my surprise, he reached over my head and pushed it closed before I could walk through it to the main part of the lodge. The next thing I knew, Troy turned me around to face him and pressed me up against that door with his firm, muscular body, showering me with delicious kisses. I couldn't move. I was trapped . . . and loving it.

Troy turned us both around and now he leaned against the door. He lifted me up with his strong arms – my feet no longer touching the floor – his hands firmly holding my butt. I looked down into his dreamy eyes with my hands around his neck. I felt so much love for this man but at this very moment I also felt lust. My body tingled, my breath quickened. Even the word *horny* entered my thoughts. Yes, I could feel my temperature rising. What's that phrase? Oh, yeah, hot and bothered.

Stop thinking, I told myself. Enjoy the feeling.

And I would have done that but a vision came to mind. One of Troy and I positioned just as we were except that he was shirtless. And, my imagination had us on the cover of a western romance novel. A giggle threatened to escape; I couldn't suppress it any longer.

Troy pulled back. "Do you want to let me in on what's so amusing?"

"Not really. Maybe later." I took his hand and led him to the large leather chair in the corner of his office. I pushed him down gently and then straddled his lap. My silly vision faded away. I initiated a do-over and resumed where we'd left off until it was time to pick up Billy.

We held hands and walked to the outer door, the main entrance to the lodge.

"I'll meet you and Billy at our residence in about an hour. Sound good?" Troy said.

"Sounds wonderful. Oh, wait. One more thing. Is there a name for the bubbly, blowing sound a horse makes when it wiggles its lips?"

"I'm not sure what you mean."

"Oh, come on. Really? It's something like this." I demonstrated the sound quite well if I do say so myself. Now Troy was the one laughing.

"That, my love, is called a *sigh*. Horses often do that when they are relaxed and happy."

"Thanks. See you later," I said stepping outside. As I grabbed Chloe's lead rope, I noticed Troy still standing in the doorway. So I sighed like a horse one more time.

BILLY WAS in rare form when I picked him up from the registration office where Saige had given him a job, chattering away non-stop.

"Mom! I got paid."

I looked at Saige and mouthed *Really?*

She nodded and said, "He was a big help and finished every task I gave him. I'm sure he'll tell you all about it."

"And I'm sure you're correct about that. Thank you."

"Bye, Miss Saige."

As soon as I set Billy back on the horse he began to give me a blow-by-blow account of his workday.

"I've got a great idea. Why don't you wait until Troy gets home? He will want to hear all about your job."

He agreed with that plan but added, "I don't want to forget about Miss Lanus."

I won't let him forget. I wanted to hear all about Miss Lanus too.

TROY BARELY MADE it through the door when Billy jumped up into his arms. "Daddy, I worked today for Miss Saige."

"And I want to hear all about that. Can we talk in the kitchen? I'd like to get our supper started. Ivy, can you set out some chips and soda? We could use a snack while Billy tells us about his day."

Apparently, Saige let Billy work in the back office with her while she worked at the computer. "She brought piles of paper books to me."

"Paper books?" Troy questioned.

"Maybe magazines?" I asked.

"Uh, huh. She called them magazines, but they were all a mess."

"What did you do with them?" Now Troy and I were both curious.

Billy explained that he studied each cover and then made better piles.

"So I made a horse pile, a cow pile, and a deer pile." He reached into his pants pocket and pulled out three quarters. "Miss Saige gave me one of these for each good pile."

"Give me five, young man," Troy said. Billy beamed with pride as he slapped Troy's hand in the air.

I had to ask, "How does Miss Lanus fit into your time with Saige?"

"I almost forgot. That's another pile for next time. And it's really big."

I was beginning to understand, but not Troy, not yet. The confused look on his face was adorable, though. So, when he turned to stir something on the stove, I stepped behind him, put my arms around his waist and whispered in his ear, "Miss Lanus is the miscellaneous, 'really big' pile."

"Thanks, babe."

. . .

THE FOLLOWING DAY, Kitchi and I had a productive one-hour meeting and came away with a wonderful plan for our special winter celebration. I informed everyone that same afternoon that it would take place the day after tomorrow at 6 p.m. in the saloon. My invitation was well-received.

Since, according to Billy, the only work I did was laundry, I had plenty of time to get ready for this event. And I enjoyed every minute of it. I even skipped my workouts and my writing for two days. However, I did manage to walk Chloe as promised.

The time flew by, and now everything was ready; the table was set with bright red candles, a pinecone center-piece, and china dishes embossed with tiny golden horse-shoes that came from our state-of-the-art kitchen. The lights were dimmed, and the fire in the river rock fire-place danced, glowed, and crackled. Tonight, the saloon was a festive winter wonderland.

I never was into much make-up, fancy clothes, or jewelry. The beautiful engagement ring Troy placed on my finger last fall was all I needed. But tonight, I wanted everything to sparkle, including myself. Highly motivated regarding my appearance, I rummaged through several unpacked boxes I had shipped from my apartment in Denver after knowing I'd be staying at the Lonely Horse Ranch with Troy.

I found a pretty white turtleneck sweater that still had the tags on it. I added a gold chain, gold hoop earrings, mascara, and light red lip color. Perfect! I still wore jeans, but it was my best pair of jeans. As a finishing touch, I sprinkled a little glitter in my hair. I may regret that in the morning.

The time had come. I was so excited to be entertaining friends for the first time in my life. Smiling, I stood with Troy and Billy just inside the double doors waiting to greet our guests.

With Kitchi's help and a few of Troy's suggestions, I created a special family-style dinner for Cody, the stable manager; the two year-round wranglers, Willy and Josh; Saige; and Charlotte, the winter housekeeper.

We insisted that Kitchi join the celebration and sit at the head of the table. His face gave nothing away, making it hard to tell if he was pleased or annoyed.

Either way, he remained in his seat until the dinner and conversation came to an end.

Saige handed Troy a short stack of mail held together with a rubber band on her way out. "Thank you both so very much," she said. "This was the highlight of my entire holiday season."

She gave me a hug and then awkwardly put out her arms to begin a hug with Troy. He met her halfway, easing her uncertainty.

"Hey, Cody. How'd you feel about walking Saige and Charlotte back to their cabins?" Troy asked.

"I'd be honored." He held out his elbows and waited for them to grab on. "Let's go for a cold, dark, winter walk, ladies."

"I think I'll go help Kitchi with the clean-up," I said. I was halfway to the hallway door – a shortcut to the kitchen – when Troy stopped me.

"Why don't you and Billy enjoy the last of the fire? I'll see if Kitchi will accept my help. You know how he is."

Yes, I did know how he was only too well. He was a strong, brave, private Native American man. While waiting for Troy to finish helping in the kitchen, Billy and I snuggled together in the oversized leather chair closest to the fireplace.

About fifteen minutes later, Troy returned, and I sensed something was wrong.

"Well?" I asked.

"Well, what?"

"Oh, I don't know. Did he let you help him in the kitchen? Did you ask about his extra days at the Wyoming property or his horse's health?" We'd both been wondering about those details.

Billy yawned and then tugged at my sweater. "Fire's

out, Mommy. We should go home to Shadow." He sounded sleepy and struggled to stay awake.

Troy seemed relieved when Billy urged us to go home. "Okay, let's go." The walk home was short, but the temperature was well below freezing, so I knew it would feel much longer than it actually was. We grabbed our coats that were hanging from rustic hooks by the door and put them on. The short stack of mail ended up in my hand, and Billy ended up in Troy's arms. Using just one hand, Troy locked both locks on the saloon door. I'd never seen him do that before, especially this time of year when so few people were around, and I wondered why.

OUR COYOTE PUP greeted us at the front door spinning around like a top and demonstrating her ever-growing ability to howl. The sound woke Billy, so Troy set him down.

"Hi, Shadow. You missed a good party," Billy said and then reached into his coat pocket, took out a dog treat, and gave it to the pup.

"You brought dog treats to the party?" I asked.

"I always have a dog treat with me. Always." Sometimes I feel like I'm talking to a little man instead of a five-year-old child. "Come on, Shadow. Let's go to bed," he said, and they scampered off.

Troy took my hand and led me to the living room of his large, modern-on-the-inside home. The exterior was as rustic looking as all the buildings here at the dude ranch. I watched him flip a switch that lit the gas fireplace and then toss in some pine chips to create a wood fire scent. At last, I'd relax on the leather sofa watching the flames flicker while Troy glanced at the mail.

"There's not much here. It seems Saige took care of most of the bills while we were gone." Troy smiled as he held up an envelope covered with cartoon stickers. "This one's for Billy."

"Billy, come back out here. You've got mail!" I called to him, smiling just as Troy was.

The boy and the pup came running. "I never got mail before. Wow! Who is it from?"

Troy handed him the letter. "Open it up and find out."

He did just that and stared at the words for a few seconds. "Yep, it's for me. I see my name." He handed the letter to me.

I looked it over and said, "It's from Lester's granddaughter, Ella. They're asking if they could come back for a winter visit in February or March." The prospect of seeing his buddy Ella again was exciting.

Billy jumped up on Troy's lap. "Can they come? Can they?"

Troy said he'd check the reservations for those two

months to see when one of the winterized cabins would be vacant.

"Come on, Billy boy. I think it's time for you and Shadow to hit the hay," Troy said.

"You're too silly, Daddy. We never hit the hay."

We let Billy and Shadow sit in one of the large leather chairs in the living room a while longer. Billy pretended to read Ella's letter to the pup while Troy and I spoke softly.

"Ivy, you never get mail, and you've been here two and half months. Doesn't anyone know where you live?"

Giving some thought to all the activity that had taken place over the past few months, I sighed heavily. Not wanting to have this conversation tonight, I chose to keep my answer simple and vague.

"I don't have any bills, and I no longer get a paycheck, so I'm not expecting mail anytime soon." I hoped that would satisfy his curiosity.

"Don't you have an older brother? Or parents? Or…"

I couldn't answer Troy's questions in front of Billy. Though I tried not to show it, Troy noticed my look of unease.

"Let's tuck Billy into bed," I said. "Then I'll fill in a few blanks."

The four of us – Billy, Shadow, Troy, and me – made our way first to the bathroom. We wouldn't be there long.

No bath tonight. I let him pick out which PJs he wanted to wear and which story he wanted to hear. The horse PJs won the toss.

"Could you both read about Clarence meeting the purple horse? That's my favorite."

Well, that was a first. One book, two readers. And so we began. We'd turned only three pages and noticed Billy was sound asleep with Shadow curled up at his feet.

I kissed him goodnight and patted the pup's head. Troy turned off the light and closed the bedroom door.

Taking my hand, he led me into the master bedroom, past his king-size bed, and into the spa – true confessions among the bubbles were about to take place. Everything about Troy's home was state-of-the-art. I doubt I could find a more luxurious spa in a five-star hotel.

I should trust Troy. We'd been through so much danger, trauma, and, yes, love together. He'd stuck by me and said he still wanted to marry me even after I told him I could not have children.

We slipped out of our clothes, tossing them onto one of the teak benches, and sank down into the hot, bubbling water. Troy had a waterproof remote to control the water temperature, the intensity of the jets, and even the music while soaking. All I had to do was tie up my hair.

Troy waited patiently for me to fill in a blank or two. I felt no pressure, which made it easier to begin.

"Yes, I do have a brother," I said with a sigh. "I tried to reach him back when we decided to be parents to Billy, remember? His number was disconnected, and there was no new number. He used to live somewhere in Pennsylvania."

Troy tilted his head and frowned. "You don't know?"

"No, I don't. But you may already know some of what I'm about to say. When I was nine years old, my brother told me that he'd be leaving home the day after his high school graduation. He and Dad never got along, and that escalated after the accident."

"He fell, right? And you watched him fall? I think you mentioned that had something to do with your fear of heights."

"Yes. That also caused the death of my parents."

"You've lost me now."

"Yeah, I'll back up a little. At the beginning of my brother's senior year, Dad signed him up for hang gliding classes. Oakley wanted no part of that, but Dad insisted. On the day of his first solo flight, something went wrong with the glider, and he came crashing down. He had multiple serious injuries but the worst one led to the loss of a leg, and I think, eventually, he lost a foot too. Life at home was miserable for everyone, and Mom never forgave Dad for making her son fly that glider."

"Ivy, I'm so sorry you had to endure such an angry, difficult environment at such a young age."

"Yeah, and that's just the half of it. Four years after the accident, there was talk of a divorce. The divorce never happened, but a murder-suicide did. Dad shot mom and then himself. Because my brother was almost twenty-two, the state let him be my legal guardian until I turned eighteen. We took care of each other, though not very well. When I turned eighteen, he moved out, and I haven't seen him since."

We climbed out of the water, dried off, and went straight to bed. We didn't speak for quite a while, just laid side-by-side under the covers, holding hands in the dark. The only illumination was a slight glimmer of moonlight peeking in the window. Every now and then, Troy would raise my hand to his lips and kiss it.

"You must think insanity runs rampant in my genes based on my childhood," I said, turning on my side to face him, wondering what his reply would be.

"No, I do not. I think you are one hell of a strong, amazing woman. It will be my pleasure to spend the rest of my life loving you and making our lives together happy and healthy forever."

CHAPTER FOUR

HANNAH

*W*earing jeans and my warm, pink hoodie, I gazed out the kitchen window at the snow-covered lower pasture and made a call.

"Hi, Ivy. It's Hannah. Is this a good time to talk?" I was surprised that she seemed to need time to think about her answer. "I can call back later if you're busy."

"No, it's fine. We didn't get much sleep last night. Had a celebration for the winter staff. If we start planning our ranch project and our weddings, I'll find my second wind. That's a promise."

I was feeling very optimistic, confident that we would do it all. I suggested we start with a brief discussion about the weddings and then develop a vision for the ranch project. Once we had that, we could set a tentative timeline.

"Ivy, since you and Troy have Billy, I think your wedding should come first."

"I appreciate your idea, but didn't you say you wanted to get married seven months after your engagement? You know, because of that Lucky Seven Curse? That would be the end of May or early June. June weddings are nice, traditional."

"I like to call it a legend. Still, that's far too soon. There's no way we could put that together and keep moving forward with our project."

"Okay," Ivy said. "Back to the ranch project. I'd definitely like to do something nice for animals."

"Maybe we could create a sanctuary for wild and domestic animals."

"Yes! And we could combine that with therapy for both animals and humans."

We were onto something. Something real. The list we'd written back in Wyoming had been long, ridiculous, and impossible. The idea of creating an old western town – a tourist attraction – was exciting but impractical. The location was too far out in the wild. No one would ever drive by or just stop in. That business would be doomed from the start.

"Hannah, I have to admit that mixed feelings are creeping in. I don't want to wait too long for Troy and me to wed."

"Then we'd better put our personal lives ahead of our ranch project."

After a few thoughtful, silent moments, we agreed on two things: We would begin a list of possible names for the ranch because The H-I Double M Ranch, though informational, just didn't cut it. And, we would hire a surveyor as soon as possible to clearly mark the property's boundaries.

Looking up at the clock above the sink, I said, "Got to go. Trace will be back from town any minute, and I'm going to surprise him with a unique trail dinner."

"Sounds interesting. Troy always cooks dinner here unless we eat in the dining hall, but I want to hear all about your trail dinner. I'll call you tomorrow."

"Okay."

Maybe I should call my invention a trail lunch rather than a trail dinner? We'd be eating it closer to midday than dinnertime. Hmm. Now that I'm thinking about it, the food I'd prepare was more like a trail snack, a three-course snack. No matter what I called it, surprising Trace would be fun.

Oatie eyed me curiously as I pushed the sofa farther from the woodstove and propped up a few pillows against it. Still, something was missing. Our backs would be fine leaning against the pillows, but our butts on the hard, wood floor? Not so fine. Then, I remembered there was an oval braided rug in the spare bedroom. I dragged it out and laid it down in front of the pillows. Oatie sat right on the middle of that rug, smiling as if I'd set that up for him.

After building and lighting a fire in the woodstove, I was ready for my cozy, indoor picnic to begin. All I needed was my handsome cowboy.

Oatie stood and wagged his tail vigorously, which was his way of telling me Trace was close by. I went to the fridge and took out the three containers holding the snacks. From there, I watched the door open. The dog greeted Trace with enthusiastic barks and a paw tapping against his leg.

Trace loved his dog; I did too. Everybody loved Oatie. "Hey, buddy," he said, patting him on his head. "What's going on in here?"

"I made a trail lunch for us that we will eat sitting on the floor in front of the woodstove," I blurted out. I watched Trace and waited for a positive sign or a word of approval. When none immediately came, I started to doubt myself. If only I could have a do-over, I'd tell him how happy I was to see him, give him a hug and a kiss, and invite him to sit down. Then I'd ask if he would like to have a trail lunch with me by the woodstove. Yes, that would've been much better.

And then he grinned, appearing more mischievous than usual. "I'll be right back. Don't go away."

"Where would I go?"

No reply came because he was too busy dashing out the door. Was he mad at me? No, he'd grinned, and that was always a good sign. While waiting for his return, I put another log on the fire and then walked from room to room, peeking out the windows, looking for signs of Trace. Never found any. He wasn't exactly *right back* by my definition of the term. Cowboy time, perhaps? No worries, I told myself. The trail lunch would not spoil or get cold – it was already cold.

Twenty minutes later, he stood on the porch just outside the doorway, stomping snow from his boots.

"We won't go far, and I'll keep you warm. That's a promise. Grab your heaviest jacket, a hat, and gloves. It's time to mount up."

I guess the surprise was on me. My cozy trail lunch would not be eaten in front of the woodstove. But where? I wondered. I tossed our snacks into a bag, and together, we rode Lewissa down past the lower pasture to the new location where, hopefully, we'd eat my trail lunch.

Trace was correct. I could actually see the roof of the house from the spot he'd picked out and set up.

"I'm impressed," I said as I dismounted Lewissa. "You did all this?"

He'd built a fire ring complete with kindling, sticks, and dead wood ready to be lit. Several layers of blankets, albeit horse blankets, covered the ground, and what appeared to be a buffalo hide set off to the side.

He must have noticed the puzzled expression on my face because he said, "It's just a little something I picked up in town this morning, although I had no idea it would be put to use so soon."

Trace lit the fire right away. I unpacked the food, which consisted of three plastic containers: one held my own version of trail mix with pecans, dried cherries, and broken sesame sticks; another was filled with cut-up carrots, radishes, and bell pepper strips; the last one contained chocolate covered strawberries. The only item holding heat was a thermos of hot green tea with lemon.

"This is perfect," Trace said as he sat next to me and threw the buffalo hide over our shoulders. It was so vast that it covered all but our faces and hands, which needed to keep free for sipping and munching.

With his hand, Trace turned my face toward his. "That was an excellent trail lunch, darlin'." He leaned in and kissed my lips, then pushed the containers away from the hide and off the blankets. Pretty sure I knew what his next move would be – lovemaking in the snow under a buffalo hide. They say there's a first time for everything.

"Are you going to tell me – as you've done in the past – that taking all our clothing off is the best way to keep warm?"

"Thought I might, but since you've already spoken those words, we can get right to it."

We laughed as we struggled to remove our clothing while remaining under the heavy hide. Troy undressed faster than me, so he gave me a hand. I'd almost caught up with his nakedness, but I insisted on wearing my socks.

Sometimes, when I was with Trace, I felt as if it were all a dream, too good to be true. With all the warnings about men my mom had given me over the years, I never expected to find love and happiness like this.

"I'm not cold at all," I said with a smile.

"The buffalo knew how to keep warm. So did the natives."

"I love you, Trace."

He laughed and tickled my face. "Are you sure about that?"

"Positive! And, it feels so good to be worry-free here at The Lucky Seven. If anyone wishes for harm to come to a McAllister, at least they are far away somewhere in Wyoming."

"I think it's time to change the subject," Trace said softly, positioning himself over me. His strong arms held his body up to keep from pressing his whole weight down onto me. I could feel the heat radiating from his skin, and I almost became too warm.

Though brief, our lovemaking today was sweet and satisfying. Trace tossed the buffalo hide to the side. We were pulling on our jeans when we were startled by three loud bangs. Lewissa spooked and took off running up the hill toward the corral, which meant we'd be walking home. I sighed as I buttoned my jeans and pulled on my boots as fast as I could. Was that gunfire that we heard? Maybe. Trace's gun appeared out of nowhere. I didn't know he'd brought it.

"That sounded like gunshots, didn't it?" I asked. "Or could that have been a vehicle up on the road backfiring?"

The serious look on his face was replaced with a subtle grin. "I'm not a hunter, but I think the only legal taking of a wild animal's life this time of year is fishing. I suppose if a fisherman ran out of worms, he might use a bullet."

Trace attempted humor, but I didn't laugh. "If you're trying to keep me from worrying, please don't. Maybe we need to be concerned." Lately, it was second nature to me to interpret unknown sounds of guns or unwanted notes from strangers as a threat or intimidation.

"It's probably nothing, but let's go home," he said. "I'll drive back down and gather up everything we left here while you have a talk with Lewissa. Your horse needs you."

We held hands as we hurried up the hill. In spite of the climb and the heat I had gathered during our love-making, I began to shiver from the cold.

Lewissa stood at the bottom of the seven steps that led up to the main door. Did she want to go in? No, of course not. What a crazy question. To my knowledge, she'd never been inside the house or climbed stairs. Still, she whinnied and pawed the ground.

"You're guarding the house, aren't you?" Lewissa and I had been through quite a bit of trauma together last fall, and I wondered if that influenced her actions today. It was almost as if she was trying to protect me from the noises we all heard. I dug into my coat pocket searching for a peppermint candy and then held out my treat-filled palm. She took it and then nuzzled my cheek with her soft nose. "You're welcome, but you can't stand here all day. Come on, let's go back to your corral. Clark misses you."

The horse did not budge; she stood her ground and refused to be tempted with another treat. Trace was already on his way down the hill to gather up the blankets, and I wanted to move Lewissa before he returned. She was in such an odd mood; I didn't dare leave her walking free. I tugged at her halter and spoke softly to her. Finally, success.

I opened the gate and led Lewissa into the arena, where she had the option of seeking the shelter of her own stall within the two-horse shed or remaining outside where she had room to run. Her friend Clark trotted over to greet her, and she seemed to relax.

As I closed the gate, I could hear the landline ringing, which was rare, so I hurried toward the house and hoped to arrive before the caller hung up.

"Hello?" I said breathlessly.

"Hi, Hannah. I've been doing a lot of thinking, and I've got some ideas to run by you," Ivy rambled. "I think they are all doable, and you're going to love them."

"Whoa, slow down, Ivy. I need to catch my breath."

"Do I dare ask why you are so breathless?" she teased.

"It's not what you're thinking. Actually, it is. I mean it was, but now it's not."

Ivy's teasing tone turned into hearty laughter.

"It's been an interesting few hours." I didn't want to talk about the loud noises right now that may or may not have been gunshots or my spooked horse. There was no need to worry Ivy about something hundreds of miles away from her. And Trace had said it was probably nothing to worry about. "I didn't expect a call from you so soon. What's up?"

"A few ideas for our timeline came to me while I was on the treadmill. Thought I'd better run them by you before they're forgotten. And then, I want you to tell me all about your trail lunch."

Well, we'd see about that. Ivy began to rattle off her ideas. I tried to listen, though she was hard to understand at times. "You're still on the treadmill, huh?"

"Yeah, I'll get off," she said. "I didn't know I'd be so out of breath."

"It seems we're both a little breathless today. Go on. I'm anxious to hear your ideas."

"Keep in mind that I don't have details yet, but as we discussed earlier, we need to hire a surveyor to clearly mark the property's boundaries right away," she said. "Next, we need to gut the old smoke-damaged barn and draw a plan or design for its new purpose."

"Okay. So far, so good. And we don't need to be in Wyoming to accomplish either of those tasks. Do you still want to create some type of animal sanctuary and eventually add animal and human therapy?"

"Yes, I do. And speaking of *I do*, the old barn could

be re-imagined and become a place for peace and joy, almost a chapel-like structure . . . if you get my drift."

I didn't. I could barely keep up with the energetic delivery of Ivy's words, but I said, "What's next on your mental list?"

"Toward the end of March, we will all meet at the property for a few days, walk the marked boundaries, and make notes of locations for the sanctuary area's fencing."

"I like all that. Just one question. Who is included in your word *all*?"

"You, me, Trace, Troy, Billy, and the dogs," Ivy said.

"What about Clint, Alice, or Kitchi?"

"It is our ranch. I'd prefer to surprise Clint and Alice after we have accomplished something. Let's bring Kitchi in at the beginning of the very next phase. Or he could make a quick trip down with Troy after we've marked off the fence locations and you've sketched a rough drawing of our ideas."

If I wanted to be part of the planning, I'd better start talking, or this would be entirely Ivy's plan. Was I resenting her take-charge attitude? I did have some ideas, though they were not well thought out yet. But she hadn't had time to do much thinking either.

So I began. "I'd like to consider having four separate sections. One for large animals, another for mid-size animals, and a small section for the small ones. Each would have its own shed to house the animals' food, supplements, and equipment needed to care for them and to shield them from severe weather. Farming could take place in the fourth area."

Ivy didn't respond to my thoughts, and that concerned me. She just went on with her remaining ideas. Was I being too sensitive?

"Kitchi could get his crew to begin work on the old barn the first half of April," she continued. "We will provide them with detailed plans before they begin. They could stay at the main house anytime they are there working until a guest house or bunkhouse is built."

I got caught up in her enthusiasm and blurted out my current two cents. "But let's get the fencing and our special peace and joy chapel structure completed first."

"Absolutely!"

At last, we worked as a team once again. I sighed with relief.

"What if we had a small, family wedding in that chapel? Surely it will be completed in time for a simple July wedding – a double wedding," I said.

Now Ivy hesitated. "Do you think our men will go along with that?"

I showed no hesitation whatsoever. "There's only one way to find out."

"You're right. And, Hannah, July is the seventh month of the year, so you'll get a seven out of it."

"And all we need to do is plan one small and simple wedding!"

We both shouted "Perfect!" at the same time. Now, if only we could have high-fived.

CHAPTER FIVE

IVY

I felt good about the plans Hannah and I had made a few weeks ago, but I was frustrated that we still hadn't come up with a suitable name for our ranch. The property had never been given an official name, so I guess there was no real rush.

Then I remembered that I hadn't asked Hannah about her trail lunch the last time we talked . . . I'd been so busy bombarding her with my ideas, I forgot. Better give her a call. This time I vowed to let her do most of the talking.

Billy was working for Saige again, so I had almost an hour all to myself. Lounging on the sofa, I tapped her number. "Hi, Hannah. Got a few minutes?"

"Sure. Just lit a fire in our woodstove. The snow is really coming down today."

"Well, I haven't forgotten about your trail lunch," I fibbed. "How did that go?"

"Uh, well—"

What was she waiting for?

"It's not a trick question. It was just lunch, though my gut tells me it might have taken place outside. You two do like to participate in the unusual."

"You're right," Hannah said. "Trace loved it – the homemade trail mix, the cut-up veggies, and a few out-of-season strawberries – and he supplied a fire, blankets, and guess what else. No, don't. You'd never guess this."

"I would have guessed a little romance under those blankets. Am I wrong about that?"

"Yes, in part. We were on top of those blankets. We were under a buffalo hide."

I laughed wildly. Hannah was right. I never would have guessed that.

"So, I take it that all's well at your Colorado Lucky Seven Ranch," I said.

"Yeah, uh, almost. There was one little glitch. During our lunch, we heard what sounded like gunshots. The sudden noise spooked my horse, and she took off running. Trace said we should get back to the house. He pretended it was no big deal and even joked that it could have been a frustrated fisherman without a worm. That's so typical of Trace."

I wondered if they had been worried at all about what they heard.

"Has anything unusual occurred at The Lonely Horse Ranch since you got back?" Hannah asked.

"No, I don't think so, but I will ask Troy to be sure. Hey, if it wasn't a fisherman, then who shot the gun? How many shots did you hear?"

"Maybe three or four. Not sure, really. It took us by surprise. If it was meant to intimidate us, the culprit succeeded. But, still, it doesn't make any sense," she said. "Unless…" She trailed off as if lost in thought. "Unless Callie was at it again trying to ruin our life together. She's had an ongoing thing for Trace and would take great pleasure in creating more chaos for us here in Colorado."

"Would she be able to conduct her mischief in Wyoming?"

I heard Hannah's heavy sigh.

"I doubt it. I'm making too big of a deal out of a few gunshots. Might have been some one trying out a new gun or having a little target practice. Besides, we know that Rudy is no longer alive, nor is his twin, Rick. But, hmm."

"What?" I needed to know because the oddness of

these mini-mysteries affected all of the McAllister family. Hannah was on to something, but what?

"Now that it's come up again, I don't recall if the lab verified a positive ID on the charred dead body found in Rick's Range Rover. I'll ask Trace to check with his friend Jane. She's Stillwater's sheriff."

"Okay. Let us know of any strange events that take place no matter how small or seemingly insignificant."

"Will do."

"Mom, can I take Shadow for a walk? We will stay right by the house. Please. Please," Billy begged.

"Okay, but only for a few minutes. In fact, how high can you count now?"

"Up to twenty-five, I think."

"Well, then. You and Shadow must be back before you finish counting to twenty-five three times. Got it? And, you must stay very close to the house. You'll need your jacket, hat, mittens, and boots."

"Aw, Mom. That'll take longer than our walk."

"Take it or leave it. Your choice." I smiled at this adorable little boy who calls me Mom. It did take him quite a while to get into his winter gear. But he did it all by himself.

"Bye, Mom." I watched him and our growing pup

walk out into the snow. "One... two... three..." He counted slowly. Sometimes he was too smart for his own good.

I did my own counting to twenty-five as I folded Billy's clothing in the laundry room. Troy insisted that his personal housekeeper take care of our laundry needs, but I insisted on taking care of all Billy's needs. I tried to mimic his slow method of counting, but when I'd counted more than six twenty-fives, I threw on my coat and boots and went to check on him and our coyote pup.

From the doorway, I called Billy's name, then I whistled for the pup. No response came from either. I ran all the way around the exterior of the house calling for my boy and the pup. Nothing. Panic set in, so I went inside and tapped Troy's office number on my cell. "I can't find Billy or Shadow," I said rapidly. "I'm going back outside to look again."

Troy rang the large, loud dinner bell attached to the dining hall's exterior wall, though not for dinner. If it rang between meals, it was an 'all hands on deck' important announcement, though that didn't amount to many hands this time of year. There was no doubt that everyone at The Lonely Horse Ranch heard the call for help. Kitchi arrived first, mere moments after the bell tolled. Cody, the stable manager, and the wranglers, Willy and Josh, soon followed.

Troy directed everyone to gather at his home just the other side of the large barn that housed his gym.

"What do we know?" Kitchi asked.

I explained the counting plan I'd devised to make sure Billy would be back inside within just a few minutes. It was a good plan. Billy understood it well, and I knew he could do it. How could he disappear and be beyond shouting distance so quickly? That was the most troubling part. All sorts of awful scenarios raced through my mind.

Hannah and I had been kidnapped in the not-too-distant past. Had Billy met the same fate? No, think positive, I repeated over and over. I did not succeed with that. There was no logical reason for his sudden disappearance. Then I remembered our encounter with the mountain lion a few months ago. Shivering, I struggled to dismiss that thought.

"Any sign of a ransom note?" Troy's tone was all business on the surface, though I heard the worry in his voice.

Kitchi offered to conduct a thorough check of the exterior of our residence, and Cody hurried back to do the same at the main lodge while I kept calling for Billy and Shadow. We all came up empty.

The men gathered near the front door of our home. Sensing that a search party was about to begin, I ran back inside to quickly throw on some warmer outerwear. Then . . . Yipping? Did I really hear yipping? I knew only one animal that made that sound.

"They've come back on their own." Thank God, I said to myself and then sighed in relief. But I was wrong. When I went back outside, dressed for the cold, my heart sank. No sign of Billy. Only Shadow had returned.

"She's trying to tell you something, Ivy." Troy stared down at the pup. He still wasn't a man who enjoyed pets, but he'd made some progress in that area since Billy came into our lives.

She jumped around, yipping all the while and then biting my boots. I picked her up, but she wiggled from my arms and ran off into the woods.

"Follow the coyote!" Cody hollered. Then, he and Willy spread out in a small search and rescue formation. Josh stayed behind in case Billy showed up. Troy, Kitchi, and I tried to follow Shadow, which was easier said than done because she zigzagged and occasionally ran circles around a tree.

We debated as to whether calling out to Billy would help or hinder the search. If he was alone and lost, calling was best. If he had been taken, this needed to be an operation of stealth. For now, stealth it was.

All of the searchers converged on a shocking scene from different directions, but at the same time. Shadow growled and showed her tiny teeth as she dashed around. I called to her, but she was busy protecting Billy in her own way. There, a man held Billy captive, gripping him tightly around his waist so his feet could not touch the ground. A woman stood at his side. Our boy thrashed and kicked but could not speak due to a gag over his mouth. I repositioned myself to the side so that he would know I was here to help him. Then I pointed to each additional rescuer but was unsure if he noticed.

The wranglers' guns were out and ready. Troy needed his hands free to rescue Billy from the man's grasp, knowing his weapon could be drawn quickly if necessary. "Put him down. Now! I'm not going to tell you again," Troy said sternly.

No one moved, and for a good reason. There was one additional person present who pointed a shotgun at the couple and Billy. We were somewhat in the line of fire too.

"Molly? Is that you?" Troy asked calmly.

We knew it was – she was the ranch's only neighbor – but we also knew her mental faculties were less than stable. She often thought she was Mary Ingalls. Caution was the only way out of this volatile situation. We also had to keep Shadow away from her. The coyote pup's canine parents lived in this troubled woman's rundown old house. If Molly grasped the connection, she would attempt to reclaim the pup. I was certain of that.

Troy didn't need to make another demand. Molly Enteman, AKA Mary Ingalls, kept her shotgun aimed at the kidnappers and, with a shaky voice, gave an unmistakable order. "Put him down or I will shoot."

Whether it was Molly's words or her old, wicked-witch appearance, they dropped Billy down to the ground and attempted to escape any gunfire or consequences for their actions.

"Not so fast," Troy said. "You don't get away with kidnapping a young child around here. Men, apprehend these two." The wranglers were happy to do that. They thrived on excitement, which was rare during the winter months. In short order, the kidnappers' hands were tied firmly behind their backs – one with a bandana, the other with a piece of rope – and they were shoved to the ground where they sat very still with angry looks on their faces.

Billy ran toward me sobbing; I met him halfway. At first, he clung tightly to my leg. We were both shaking. "You're going to be all right. You're safe now," I said softly while separating him from my leg. I knelt down and removed the gag those despicable people had tied over his mouth. He reached up to put his arms around my neck. Standing now, I held Billy in my arms and slowly backed farther away from the guns still drawn. If only I had a few more hands, I would pick up Shadow too. On the pup's third attempt to jump up, Kitchi appeared and caught her. She was content in his arms. They, too, had a powerful bond.

Troy radioed the one remaining wrangler who'd stayed behind at the ranch. "Call the cops. They need to make an arrest ASAP. We're located about halfway between our western boundary and Molly Enteman's old place."

I could not keep silent. I had to know why these two people tried to kidnap Billy. Was it only to hurt Troy or me or the McAllister family in general? Were they the same people who left the intimidating note in Wyoming?

With Billy in my arms, his head buried on my shoulder and puffing warm sobs onto my neck, I kept my distance but asked my questions.

"Who are you, and why are you here?" I practically yelled at them. The man and woman looked at each other but said nothing. "Do you realize there are four guns pointed at you?"

The woman snarled, exposing her rotten teeth. "He's my child, not yours. You did not conceive him or give birth to him." More angry words seethed through her clenched jaw. "I am his mother!"

Billy popped his head up and yelled, "You're not my mommy. You're just a bad lady."

Of course, the woman could be his biological mother; we'd learned from Troy's lawyer that her rights to Billy had been terminated when he was a toddler due to her numerous criminal activities, drug use, and child endangerment. The list of her offenses was long.

Molly, still aiming her shotgun toward the couple, snapped, "Give everything back."

I wondered what she meant. Had this couple stolen something from her too? Then, she slowly moved her gun and took aim at Troy, making the air around us quiver with turbulent emotion. Suddenly a light went on, and I finally understood.

I stepped closer to Troy. "Biomom wants Billy, and I'll bet Molly wants Shadow," I whispered, shaking his arm.

He nodded, never taking his eyes from gun-toting Molly. "Well, then, neither will get what they want. I'll make certain of that."

He nudged me and pointed to a pine tree about ten feet from where we stood. He wanted Billy and me away from him. He didn't need to explain why. *God, I love this man.*

The wranglers had control over the kidnappers, so they were no longer an immediate problem, but would this incident cancel our pending adoption of Billy? The caseworker was one tough cookie. Would we be viewed as unfit parents because I let Billy go outside alone, allowing this kidnapping to occur? What would the future bring?

I heard the sound of a vehicle, probably off-road quads of some kind. That was quick. Perhaps they were already nearby. Then another thought occurred to me. "I hope that's law enforcement . . . and not the kidnappers' back up," I said to myself.

Two quads roared up, each driven by our local deputies; Troy and I had recently met them. Molly turned and pointed her shotgun at them as they slammed on their brakes. They quickly matched her threat with their own handguns. Now, with six guns drawn, I wanted to get Billy out of there. What must be going through his little head?

He opened his tightly closed eyes and looked up when he'd heard the vehicles arrive. Taking it all in, he asked, "Are we in trouble?"

"No, sweetie. The people that took you are in big trouble, and the old lady is in a little trouble. We're okay, and we'll be heading home soon." I prayed that was true.

I watched the two officers and Troy spread out. If Molly were to fire her shotgun, the bullets would fly in one general direction first, and two out of the three men would apprehend her. Hopefully, it wouldn't come to that.

Then again, perhaps she was a poor shot. I prayed for that scenario too.

Then, it occurred to me that her presence here in the woods with her shotgun had saved Billy. If she hadn't been out walking in the woods today, the kidnappers would be long gone with our boy. The officers needed to know that.

I called out to Molly but got no response of any kind from her. Then I remembered that sometime in the past, she had taken on the identity of Mary Ingalls, the older sister of Laura Ingalls Wilder. She must have read about the Ingalls family and Little House books too when she was younger.

"Mary! Mary Ingalls?" I called to her again using a gentle tone.

Ah, that worked. The woman turned toward me. "I want to thank you for saving our boy's life, Mary. Those bad people were going to steal him. Do you think you could put down your gun for a few minutes? The boy would like to come closer to thank you too, but your big gun is scaring him."

"Oh," was all she said at first as she lay the gun on the snow-covered ground. "I see the light now."

Troy walked slowly toward her with open arms. She accepted his hug. One of the officers picked up her shotgun. "It's not loaded," he said in a hushed voice, apparently not wanting to upset this unstable woman.

Hearing those words, Billy and I went to join Troy to help keep Molly calm and distracted while the officers removed the kidnappers. We didn't need another kidnapping . . . or rather, a dognapping.

Kitchi, who was still holding Shadow, and the other wrangler walked back to our Lonely Horse Ranch with Billy and me. Troy and Cody remained at the scene until it was put to bed, and Molly was safely back inside her old house with her coyote family, minus one.

Hannah

Ivy and I often spoke about our ranch project as well as our wedding plans. I felt terrible for her and the near kidnapping of Billy. I couldn't get over how stressful that must have been. Then, an interesting thought occurred to me. So I called her, even though the hour was late.

"Hannah, what's wrong?"

We'd all grown accustomed to problems. Some days, trouble seemed to be the norm.

"Nothing."

"Oh, well, that's a relief."

"An idea just now came to mind, and I wanted to run

it by you, though I realize you may already have thought of this."

"Don't keep me in suspense, Hannah. Just spit it out."

"What if Billy's biological mother and her accomplice – or was he the bio dad? – were the arsonists and the authors of the note we received the day we left Wyoming? If so, that would mean our troublemakers were out of the way for at least a few years."

"You could be on to something. I hope you're right. That would be an enormous weight taken from all of our shoulders."

"Were you ever told where Billy was born or where his original home was?"

Ivy paused. Thinking, I assumed.

"Not sure, but Billy's uncle lived in Oregon and he could have been biomom's brother, but I don't know. I do know that he backed out of the deal to keep Billy at the last minute. I wonder if biomom threatened him. I guess I still have more questions than answers. I do love your idea, though, and perhaps we really can stop being on the lookout for trouble. My neck is sore from looking over my shoulder many times each day."

I was sure that Ivy would mention our conversation to Troy; I would do the same with Trace. Hopefully, that would allow us to relax a bit and enjoy life on the ranch.

After we hung up, I realized I'd neglected to mention

that March was fast approaching, which meant it was time to set a date for all of us to head back to Wyoming to our new, though very old ranch. We'd all agreed to do that. The surveyor had completed his part. After we arrived, we'd walk the marked property lines, and based on the shape and terrain of that land, rough out the next plan of action.

THE BFF, THE MAGIC WHISTLE, & THE TROUBLESOME POT

CHAPTER SIX

IVY

$\mathcal{I}$t was time to confirm a date for Lester and Ella's visit. I did think their request to visit our Montana ranch during February or March was unusual. The weather would still be cold and snowy.

"Troy, did you check with Saige about the availability of one of our cozy, winterized cabins? Lester and Ella want to come for a visit, remember?"

"I not only remembered, I spoke with Lester this morning. They are all set for a one-week stay beginning on February 21st."

"Yay," Billy cheered as he and Shadow dashed out from the boy's bedroom.

"Were you listening to our conversation?" I asked.

"Not until I heard Ella's name. Am I in trouble?"

"What do you think, Troy?"

"I think both of you should let me finish telling my tale."

Billy and I nodded, eager to hear what he had to say.

"They have something to celebrate, and they want to do that here with us."

"Tell us, hurry. I can't wait." Billy hopped up and down with excitement.

"Okay. Once upon a time, there lived a little girl named Ella who—"

I groaned, and Billy continued his antsy behavior. "Just tell us, Mr. Storyteller, before we explode," I pleaded.

"If you're going to be that way," he said with a wink, "I'm going into the kitchen for some sparkling water. You want anything?"

We shook our heads.

"Okay. Here's the gist. Lester will soon have full custody of his granddaughter, Ella." He wigged his eyebrows, turned, and headed to the kitchen.

"Wow! So she's my sister now?" Billy asked with sweet innocence.

"No." What could I say that wouldn't crush him? "But, she could be your BFF."

"Huh?"

"BFF. Best. Friends. Forever. Wouldn't that be wonderful?"

I had crushed him, although his sad little face held a thoughtful look too.

"What if I want to love her?" Staring up at me, he waited for my answer.

"Troy! I could use a little help out here."

A FEW PLEASANT, trouble-free winter weeks flew by. And now, we expected that Lester and Ella would arrive today. I'd never seen Billy quite so hyper. You'd think it was Christmas all over again.

"Mom," he called from his bedroom. "I need your help."

There was no evidence of distress in his voice, so I cheerfully replied, "I'm on my way."

Billy had three pairs of pants and even more shirts set on his bed. "I can't decide what to wear."

He looked so happy and yet so serious at the same time. "Hmm. Do you want to impress Ella with a cowboy look or something more traditional?"

"What's Dad going to wear?"

"I don't know, sweetie. But if he has any clothing other than western wear, I've never seen it."

I heard the landline ringing and turned to Billy. "Are you good with making your own decision?"

He nodded. "Yep. I got this."

So I hurried to answer the phone. "Hello?"

"Hi, Ivy," Saige said. "They're all checked in and walking over to their cabin."

"Do you want me to ask one of the wranglers to help with their luggage? Right now, Troy's in the woods doing something with Shadow. Said he wouldn't be long, but when a cowboy is with a coyote out in the woods, I'm sure keeping track of time is not a priority."

"Well, they didn't bring much with them. They're fine, just anxious to see all of you. Especially Billy."

"That doesn't surprise me. Billy has been bouncing off the walls all day long, asking if they're here yet every few minutes. I'll let Kitchi know that we'll have dinner in the dining room tonight. Thanks, Saige. Maybe we'll see you there?"

Saige's answer was slow in coming. "Um, okay. I guess I could do that. You know what? I'll be there. In fact, I wouldn't miss this reunion for the world."

I asked her to stop by Lester's cabin – it was close to her office – and let him know we would meet him and Ella in the saloon in about an hour.

Right after I hung up the phone, I heard a noise at the

back entrance. My cowboy and the coyote must have returned.

"Anybody home?" Troy called out. "We need a couple of old towels."

The man has no old towels. I grabbed two of the darkest colored towels I could find knowing Troy likes the light ones, especially the white ones, for use in the spa.

"You're both covered in mud," I said as I walked into the mudroom with the towels.

"Thanks for stating the obvious," he said as he stripped off his clothing. "That's why we entered through the mudroom."

I tossed him the towels. He wrapped one around his waist and the other around Shadow.

"How did you get so muddy when the ground is covered with snow?"

"Not all the ground is snow-covered. We're living proof of that. Do you want to wash Shadow while I shower?"

"Nope. We're meeting Lester and Ella in the saloon in less than an hour, and I need to get Billy and myself ready for that. Why don't you both jump in the shower?"

"I'd rather shower with you than a muddy coyote pup." He winked.

"Later, handsome."

· · ·

KITCHI MUST HAVE KNOWN we would meet Lester and Ella in the saloon, though I don't remember telling him about that. Maybe Troy did. It didn't matter because I was delighted with what I saw. Tiny white lights twinkled, and bright orange flames danced in the fireplace. A plate arranged with crackers, cheese, and grapes was set out, as well as a bowl of freshly popped popcorn. An ice bucket containing sparkling water and orange soda stood off to the side. Now, all we needed was Lester and Ella to walk through—

The door flew open, and then the two kids squealed and ran to each other. I gave Lester a hug before Troy shook his hand.

"Let's all sit, have a snack, and get reacquainted until dinner is ready," I suggested.

I didn't know if Ella was aware of the custody issue and hoped Billy wouldn't say anything about it until after Lester brought it up.

"I brought you a gift." The little girl handed Billy a package shaped like a book.

He looked at me with a panic-filled face. Oh, dear. Our little guy had nothing for her. I could come up with something tomorrow, but not tonight.

I looked at Troy, hoping he'd figured what was happening and come up with a plan.

"Why don't you open Ella's gift, Billy, while I go get

your gift for her," Troy said.

"Okay," he said with an uncertain tone.

Neither Billy nor I had a clue what Troy was up to, and he was certainly taking his time.

Billy opened his present. It was an album that included photos of Ella's stay at the ranch last year and pictures she'd drawn and colored herself. They sat side by side as Ella gave him a guided tour through the album. A good distraction from his concern about the gift he didn't have for her.

Troy returned with a small package. He handed it to Billy so he could be the one to present it to Ella.

"Thank you for the book, Ella. I really like it." He looked at the small, wrapped package he held in his hand. Shyly, he gave it to Ella. "I hope you like it."

Even though he didn't understand all of it, I was so proud of him for going along with this last-minute, impromptu plan.

"Go ahead. Open it, Ella," I said, curious to know what Troy had come up with.

She took her time carefully removing the bow and then the wrapping paper. Then she stared at the box containing her present.

"Open it, Ella," Lester said urging her on. "We all want to see what's in it."

"I will. I'm trying to imagine what it is."

Oh, my gosh. Billy and Ella are like two peas in

a pod.

At last, she lifted the lid from the box. With her eyes wide open, she nodded and said, "It's so pretty. It's silver. Thank you, Billy." She blew on it, but there was no sound.

"Billy got you a magic whistle," Troy said. "People can't hear it, but animals can. I'll show you how to use it tomorrow, okay?"

Kitchi poked his head into the saloon. "Dinner is served."

THE HALF DOZEN ranch guests were seated at one of the smaller dinner tables and had begun passing the bowls of food around. Meals in the dining hall were often served family-style.

"Can we sit with the cowboys?" Billy asked as the minimal winter staff straggled in. Without waiting for Troy's answer, he turned to Ella. "Is that okay with you?"

"Oh, yes. But I have to ask my dad if that's okay with him. He used to be grandpa, but now he's my dad."

The little girl's comment answered one of my questions. The full-custody issue was definitely not a secret, though I'd refrain from making any comments until Lester made his official announcement.

Smiling up at Lester after asking if she could sit with

the cowboys, Ella took Billy's hand. "Come on, Billy," she directed as they headed toward the staff table.

Troy, Lester, and I joined them. It wasn't long before Saige sat down across from us, told the kids how happy she was to eat dinner with them, and began passing around the bowls and platters piled high with food.

"Eat up, everyone. Beef stew is one of Kitchi's best winter meals. And the homemade bread will melt in your mouth," Saige said.

Her plate, however, was almost devoid of the delicious food. Even Troy noticed that and asked, "Not hungry tonight, Saige?"

"Just saving room for later," she said. "I'm having a visitor, and we'd planned a late-night dinner in my cabin."

"I hope your visitor is not a paying guest at the ranch," Troy stated softly.

"Oh, no. I would never do that. I know the rules."

"Then who?" Troy asked insistently.

I couldn't hold back and jabbed my elbow into Troy's side. "She's entitled to a private life, you know," I whispered. "And we broke all the rules last fall."

"Miss Saige," Billy said, "Is he your BF?"

Ella giggled. "I think you left out an F. Didn't you mean BFF?"

Appearing confused, Saige looked from Billy to Ella

to me. Had she never heard that term before?

"The kids are talking about best friends forever, otherwise known as BFF."

"Thanks, Ivy. I get it now."

Billy wasn't finished making his point, though. "So, Miss Saige, if your visitor is your BFF, you can't love him."

Saige looked confused again. The poor woman. I was pretty sure she was beginning to regret joining us for dinner.

"Who's ready for dessert?" Saige said as she stood up from the table. "It's Kitchi's famous chocolate mousse."

I had to laugh as the confusion shifted from Saige to Billy.

"I never saw a chocolate moose and I'm not going to eat one . . . unless it's like a chocolate Easter bunny."

CHAPTER SEVEN

HANNAH

*I*t was nearly March 18th, the day Ivy and I had chosen for all of us to return to the ranch in Wyoming. We planned to accomplish our initial tasks in just four days. Kitchi was an integral part of the actual construction, so he'd come too but was willing to stay only one night this trip. Sometimes I didn't understand that man. We'd make it work, though.

Troy and Ivy would take our completed plans back to him. Only the five of us would make this trip. No, how could I have been so wrong? Troy and Ivy would bring Billy, probably Shadow, and at least one horse too. Clint and Alice would remain in Golden, Colorado, at their condo. We'd inform them of our progress along the way.

Standing at the kitchen counter packing some food items into a crate, I felt Oatie's paw on the back of my leg.

"Good morning, Oatie. I suppose you want to come too."

This poor dog, amazing as he was, had been through the mill. First, he sustained serious injuries when my kidnapper threw a metal wrench at him just before riding off with me, and two months later, he was accidentally shot when he was mistaken for an attacking wolf.

"Here, Oatie." I handed him one of his favorite treats and rubbed his head. "You know, if we bring you to Wyoming with us, you must not be a hero this time."

He'd also injured his hind leg when he went flying over a cliff while searching for Clint. He's still healing from TPLO (tibial plateau leveling osteotomy) surgery.

"You and your pup, Little Charlie, will be indoor dogs for the duration of this trip." He whined as I pretended he knew exactly what I'd said.

I carried all the smaller, lighter items to the truck while Trace loaded up hay and grain for Beauty, the horse he chose to bring this time. Actually, being a Spanish Barb, I learned that her legal name was Hermosa de Dragoon.

"Trace, why do you call her Beauty?"

"After a year of many horse people saying things like, 'She's a real beauty,' I gave in and called her Beauty too. Hermosa and beauty have similar meanings. It works."

I didn't know this horse very well. I'd only seen her once, the day I'd selected Blackjack to be Trace's horse for his dad's Wyoming Challenge. She'd been trailered down from The Big Mack to The Lucky Seven yesterday. She was a beautiful chestnut-colored horse with a tri-colored blonde mane and tail – blonde, copper, and light brown. She was almost as pretty as my palomino mare, Lewissa. Of course, I might be a bit biased.

We'd be mostly packed up today, so we could head out early tomorrow. Feeling hopeful that this would be a danger-free outing with family – something rare in our short time together – I couldn't wait to get there.

"Are you ready for a break, darlin'?"

I loved the sound of Trace's voice. I loved everything about him, but I must have turned toward him far too quickly because I suddenly felt faint. This was an affliction I had had since my teenage years, but such a feeling has been rare lately. Luckily, my cowboy wrapped his arms around me in the nick of time.

"I guess you do need a break, though a simple nod or a yes would have been sufficient," he teased. "Let's go sit on our favorite bench by the corral for a few minutes."

"I'd like that." It was on that bench that Trace had proposed and placed the beautiful, horseshoe-shaped ring on my finger. "And we can spend time with my horses, Lewissa and Clark. Will Harry check on them while we're gone?"

"Every day."

"Good. Then I won't worry about them in our absence."

"We won't worry about anything. Our troubles are in the past," Trace assured me.

More than a few minutes had passed. Trace leaned in and kissed me on the lips right before scooping me up in his arms. He'd become a fantastic kisser among other delightful, breathtaking talents. I took in the delicious scent that lingered on his warm, tan neck as he carried me inside. I tingled with excitement, knowing I was about to receive a sample of some of those talents.

He set me down gently on the bed and then escorted Oatie and Little Charlie from the room. Turning to me, he smiled.

"No dogs allowed right now," he said as he clicked the door closed.

Still, we could hear them snorting and puffing the other side of the door. That was a bit distracting, and we spent the next few minutes attempting to muffle our laughter. Eventually, the dogs must have fallen asleep or become bored with us and moved to another room. Either way, my attention was now on Trace as he slowly undressed me, kissing me all the while. Laughter was the furthest thing from my mind.

CHAPTER EIGHT

IVY

Turning off the paved road onto the dirt road was more challenging than we'd expected. The snow was much deeper than it had been in December, and we were the first to make tracks in the pristine whiteness. With its beauty came spinning tires and a fish-tailing horse trailer.

"That's what we get for arriving first." I punched Troy's coat-covered bicep. "You know there is no reward this time, right?"

"Very funny. Oh, wait. I think there might be if we hurry." He winked, then looked straight ahead with both hands gripping the wheel as he maneuvered the truck and trailer toward the cabin.

I knew exactly what he meant, but there was no way to pull off what he had in mind. I appreciated the thought, though. We had Billy, Shadow, and a horse that needed attention and to get settled in. Hopefully, Troy's horse, Tracker, would tolerate the charred barn next to the cabin. The forecast was for extremely cold nights during our stay, too cold even for a Montana horse.

I took Billy and Shadow inside, got them settled, and then I built a fire in the woodstove. This ancient stove gave off an amazing amount of heat. The living area would be warm enough in less than an hour.

"Billy, you're in charge of Shadow. Do not let her out." After her solo romp in the woods during Billy's kidnapping, I couldn't take the chance of the coyote pup hearing the call of the wild and being overcome with curiosity. No, until everyone else arrived – Trace, Hannah, Oatie, and Little Charlie – Shadow needed to stay close to Troy or me whenever she went outside.

As I warmed my hands near the woodstove, I heard Troy shouting, Tracker squealing, and lots of kicking and stomping. "I'll be right back, Billy. Stay! Don't even open the door."

"Can I look out the window?"

"I suppose so," I said as I rushed outside. Now, I wished I hadn't granted him permission to look out. What if it wasn't a pretty sight?

"Troy, what's the problem?"

"Tracker refuses to go in. Not even a bribe of alfalfa worked."

I walked into the barn to see if there was anything that could be spooking Tracker. It still reeked of burnt wood and smoke. "Your horse wants nothing to do with fire," I called from inside. "Who can blame him? It's awful, disgusting. We brought his blanket, right?"

"Yeah. I'll go get it."

"I will open up all the doors and windows if I can. Maybe it will air out enough to please him. Your horse is used to five-star accommodations. This burnt old barn gets zero stars."

Together, we put the blanket on Tracker and tied him to the trailer with an extra-long lead rope.

"Ivy, I hear a truck headed this way. It must be Hannah and Trace."

I knew they'd struggle driving the last leg of the journey as we had, and it would take them a while. So Troy and I used the extra minutes to unload the items that were needed inside, and switch all the fuses in the fuse box to the On position . . . and say a little prayer that everything electrical worked.

Voila! We had light, a working refrigerator, and I could hear the pump's motor rumbling, so we'd soon have water too. I checked the stove, Troy's favorite appliance.

"The stove isn't working, Troy." That was not a good way to begin our short, busy visit here.

He frowned, looked at me, and then at the stove. After turning every knob, he scratched his head. "Must be out of propane."

"Does that mean no cooking on the stove? For four days?"

I hoped I was wrong about that. Our time here would be miserable without hot food. We all loved to eat, especially Troy's cooking.

"If we want a working stove and hot water, we need some propane."

"Are you sure? The stove was working when we left in December. There's likely a logical explanation for the lack of propane, right?"

"Oh, yeah. There is. The tank must have been drained because it was half full when we left." Troy began to pace with a look of worry and anger on his face.

I didn't like the feeling of paranoia that suddenly surged through me. Shake it off!

"Maybe the property manager assumed no one would be here, and, trying to be helpful, decided to drain it." My comment had little effect on my negative feelings or Troy's anger.

He shook his head and stomped from the kitchen. I listened and overheard his cell phone call to Kitchi – by some miracle, it went through even though we were close to the middle of nowhere. He asked the man to bring a few portable tanks of propane with him. The sooner, the better.

Not wanting to make Troy's day worse than it already was with my questions, I snuck a call to Kitchi. Crossing my fingers, hoping for a little luck, he answered.

"Hi, Kitchi. It's Ivy. Got one more thing to run by you." I informed him of the horse's issue with the charred barn. "The temperature will dip below zero tonight. I'm worried."

"Did you bring two horses?"

"No, but Trace will be here any minute with one of his horses."

"Good. Park your trailer next to the barn's south wall. Put their coats on, and then get them in the trailer before the sun goes down. They'll keep each other warm."

"Thanks." I hung up just in time to get Billy and Shadow and join Troy as he greeted Hannah and Trace.

We had a few joyful minutes watching the dogs and Billy romping in the snow before we helped them unload. After that, we informed them of the current propane situation.

We were a resourceful group, though. Together, we

turned our propane problem into an opportunity. We had a real cookout, outside over a wood fire. This worked quite well, except for the fact that the cooks were cold.

Sleeping was a different story. I could hear the stomping and neighing of the unhappy horses out in the trailer from our bedroom. Even Troy, a sound sleeper, got up several times to check on them. I kept telling myself that tomorrow would be better for everyone.

KITCHI ARRIVED BY 10 A.M. We gave him waves and smiles just for showing up and a standing ovation for bringing the small propane tanks Troy had requested. Now, if only they could figure out how to hook them up to the stove and hot water heater.

Kitchi had opened the horse trailer's side door to remove the propane tanks, and I saw something else. Curious, I had to say, "You brought a gas grill too? What's the plan for that?"

"It's always good to have a backup plan."

Troy said, "You brought a horse trailer, but no horse."

Trace frowned, and Troy shifted his weight from one boot to the other. Seeing both men baffled was a rare sight, indeed. Opening the back of the trailer, we all saw it was filled with lumber.

"We're beginning construction today?" Trace asked. "Isn't it a little premature for that?"

"No, we are building a temporary shelter for your horses," Kitchi said with a subtle smile my way. "We just need two sides and a roof. With your help, it should be done before lunchtime."

The guys went to work using one exterior side of the stinky old barn. Saws buzzed, hammers pounded.

After several trips to and from the cabin, we'd completed the task of bringing in the items that were still in our trucks.

"Hannah, you're so good with horses. Do they seem agitated to you?" I asked. With all the noise so close by, I was a little agitated myself.

"I don't know what's normal for Beauty or Tracker, but yes, I see signs that could be mild agitation. Let's walk them up the long dirt road. The snow is already packed down from our vehicles, so it won't be a difficult walk."

"Sounds good. I'll grab two lead ropes."

"Ivy, what do you want to do about Billy?"

The men were focused on the shed project and their power tools, not on a five-year-old child. No way would I let him out of my sight.

"I'll get him, and he can sit on Tracker. He'll love that." I retrieved his saddle pad from the trailer, put it on the horse's back, and set my bundled-up boy on top of it. "You can hold on to his mane, okay? Hannah and I will make sure we all go slow."

We left the canines back in the cabin. We devoted all of our attention to the horses, Billy, and the beauty of the winter wonderland that surrounded us. Our feet crunched on the sparkling snow, and the horses' hooves plodded, sinking down to the frozen ground. With the sun shining, combined with our activity, we stayed warm, almost too warm. We kept walking. And Billy hummed a tune.

Softly, I asked, "Is he humming 'Beer for My Horses'?"

"It does sound similar to that song. At least he's not singing the words." We both laughed.

"Troy sings a few songs at the Friday Night Cook-outs. That might have been one of them."

When the sounds of construction ceased, we stopped too and gave Billy, the horses, and ourselves peppermint treats. But I noticed that Hannah wasn't her usual self today. So I had to ask, "Are you okay?"

"Sure. I'll be fine. I'm just tired." She sighed and leaned up against Beauty. "I didn't sleep well last night and with all packing and—" Her voice trailed off.

I knew she wasn't a gym rat like me, and I didn't expect her to be as physically strong, but she'd always had sweet, positive energy that radiated all around her. That was not the case today.

"Why don't you ride your horse? I can easily hold two lead ropes."

"She's not my horse, and I don't know her very well. I'd give her a try, but there is no way I can get up on her back from the ground, especially with no saddle."

I glanced around. There sat a perfectly shaped rock as if it was meant for mounting a horse. "Come on. You can do this."

Once up on Beauty's back, Hannah seemed pleased and relieved. We all enjoyed our walk – or ride – back to the cabin and our men.

The horses' temporary shed was as complete as it was going to get. I helped Billy dismount, and Trace, placing his hands around his lady's waist, helped Hannah down. When I unclipped the lead ropes, each horse found its way to one of the large water buckets and then to a rough-sided trough filled with fresh hay and a bit of alfalfa. Neither horse seemed to care about dominating the other. We had happy horses once again, acting like old friends.

"I don't see Troy. Where he'd go?" I hoped he hadn't begun to walk the property without me.

"He's inside setting up a late lunch for all of us,"

Trace said, grinning. That cowboy was a grinner. If Troy did that, I'd be suspicious.

"Great! Let's eat." I couldn't wait to get going. The sun would dip below the hills on the horizon in about three hours, and we'd want to be back at the cabin shortly after that.

THE FARTHER we went from the dirt road, the deeper the snow. Little Charlie and Shadow were literally in over their heads. It was a challenge for the rest of us too. We hadn't expected quite this much snow so late in March. Trace took the small animals back to the cabin to stay with Oatie. He returned with the two horses and led them ahead of us to pack down the snow. What a difference that made. Even Billy managed to walk on his own, no riding or carrying necessary.

Troy knew the length of his stride, so he counted his steps between each marker, and we calculated the distance. Hannah, the closest thing we had to an architect, sketched a miniature, close-to-scale drawing of the information as it became available. We noted trees, bushes, an old stock tank, and a small, mostly frozen stream.

Kitchi took photos of everything. Even though he didn't say much, I knew his brain was busy thinking and doing some of its own calculations.

Back at the cabin, Kitchi remained outdoors for a while taking photos of the exterior and charred interior of the small old barn. Billy fell asleep at the dinner table. Fortunately, I sat right next to him and was able to stop the sleepy child from face-planting into his plate of fettuccini.

Troy sensed that I needed some help. "I got this," he said, picking Billy up and winking.

He was a winker. I'd been with the brothers long enough to know that Trace was the grinner and Troy was the winker. And both men often used the phrase, *I got this*.

Before long, Billy slept soundly in his bed, and we sat comfortably in the living area watching the fire and discussing the day's accomplishments.

Hannah and I shared most of our ideas for our ranch project, but we hadn't yet broached the connection between the project's construction schedule and our wedding thoughts.

Kitchi took notes during the conversation but then abruptly said, "I must leave tomorrow."

Troy didn't seem surprised, he expected Kitchi's stay to be very short, but I knew he wished it wasn't true. Still, he was curious. "Why? What's going on?"

"Got some things to do."

That was so like Kitchi – a very private man. When

he stood and walked back into the kitchen, I followed him.

"Since you're going to miss hearing some of our ideas, desires, and plans, I want you to know that we'd like to turn the old barn into a rustic but beautiful chapel-like place for meditation, quiet time, a reading corner, and . . . our double wedding."

Kitchi listened but offered no comment. Not even a nod. Was this going to be a problem? Were we asking too much?

"Hannah and I have agreed to have a small, family wedding right here. What do you think about that?" I waited for a reply, or even an expression would do. When my impatient pause felt awkward, I continued. "Just so you know, Trace and Troy aren't aware of this yet. But they will be before we turn out the lights and say goodnight."

Leaving him in the kitchen, I returned to the living area without mentioning the second part of our plan – creating a similar but outdoor mini-sanctuary. A calm, restful place where one or two animals could be brought to visit now and then. It would butt up against one wall of the rebuilt barn. Since Kitchi seemed uninterested in any sort of conversation, I decided to wait until we were back at The Lonely Horse Ranch to bring that up.

Just as I sat down by the woodstove so I could pet the

pets, Hannah spoke up. "There's another pressing topic at hand – our weddings."

I wondered how much she and Trace had discussed this, if at all. We hadn't come to a definite decision, but we had some darn good ideas.

Hannah's comment seemed to energize our men. Trace jumped right into the wedding discussion. "Don't keep us in suspense. We guys value a decent lead time, you know."

The two men glanced at each other and nodded ever so subtly. "Trace is correct, and we want to make sure you each have the wedding you desire."

I wasn't surprised at the men's comments. They were both wonderful men. Hannah and I felt fortunate to have them in our lives in spite of the bizarre activities that occurred since we hooked up. They were crazy-mad in love with us and we with them. The only downside for me was that I may never get the great American novel written, which was my original reason for venturing to The Lonely Horse Ranch.

"You'll have plenty of lead time, I'm quite sure," Hannah insisted, seeing a hint of concern on Trace's face. "Kitchi will get a crew started on rebuilding the old barn, turning it into a beautiful place of contemplation, peace, and joy."

"So the barn will no longer be a barn?" Troy said with a frown.

"Correct. We won't need that barn." I smiled and moved over to sit on Troy's lap. "Want to know why?"

Before he answered, I kissed him on the mouth.

"Are you trying to soften me up before you deliver the no-barn blow?" he asked and then winked.

"No softening needed. You're going to love our wedding plan."

"Yeah, but what about the—"

I put one finger to his lips. "Shh! Hannah, help me out here."

Hannah smiled, though her eyes looked sleepy. It had been a long day.

"Well, gentlemen. I'll get right to the point." She was happy to help despite her sleepiness. "We will have a small, beautiful double wedding, and it will take place in our newly remodeled barn."

"That's right, and Kitchi knows to begin that project first. After that, some of the fencing and the new barn at the center of the three animal sanctuary sections will go up."

"Whoa!" Trace shook his head. "Ladies, I'm having trouble understanding your vision."

"I'm with you, brother. Sounds complicated and expensive."

"Don't worry, guys. We've got this," I said. Hannah and I shared a grin and a wink, finishing with a giggle.

"Ivy's right. Once we walk the rest of the property, I'll be able to create an approximate drawing of our vision. Then your concerns will fade away."

Looking from man to man, I asked, "But you're okay with the double wedding, yes?" I waited impatiently for a reply, hoping for a grin and a wink. No luck there. Eventually, they each shrugged and nodded. Good enough for me. "Great!"

We'd all had a long day and agreed it was bedtime. Billy had been asleep since dinner, and the pets were curled up in front of the fire, all eyes closed. The canines needed a quick trip outside before we officially tucked in for the night. I volunteered to take them out. Hannah went to the kitchen to make some chamomile tea, asking if anyone else wanted some. There were no takers.

"Come on, pups, last call." Little Charlie, Shadow, and Oatie rose up and stretched before slowly making their way to the front door. The night air was cold but still, and a wintry silver moon shone brightly above. The scent of properly burning logs in the woodstove drifting upward was the icing on this evening's cake. I could have remained outside longer, but I noticed all the pets were standing at the door. So much for the peace and quiet the frosty night offered.

I heard a noise over by the horses' temporary stall. It wasn't made by a horse. It was a human sound, a cough or clearing of one's throat.

"Hello?" I called. "Who's there?"

I heard footsteps coming from the shadows, heading in my direction, and wished I'd brought a flashlight.

"Miss Ivy. Good evening."

"Kitchi?" I still couldn't make out who it really was, though Kitchi was the only person who called me Miss Ivy.

"What are you doing?"

"Just checking on the horses and walking the cabin's perimeter. Can't be too careful nowadays."

I should have known if there was a problem, the dogs would not have stayed sitting quietly by the door.

"Thank you, Kitchi. Good night."

I walked back inside and found the living room empty, so I went about the task of banking the fire. I knew Shadow would find Billy and sleep with him. Oatie and Little Charlie chose to curl up by the woodstove again. Just as soon as I filled up the dogs' water dish in the kitchen, I'd snuggle into bed with Troy.

Approaching the kitchen doorway, I came to a sudden stop, not believing what I saw. The man, soon to be my husband, had his arms wrapped around Hannah, her head on his chest. Shocked and speechless, I held my breath as

I backed away. How could this be happening? I did not see this coming. I fought an unexpected urge to fight back, rush in there and catch them in the embrace, let them know they'd been caught . . . or maybe I should pay Trace a visit. Turnabout is fair play, right? What is the matter with me? No, no, my thinking is flawed. I should be asking, what's the matter with them?

TROY WAS ALREADY in the kitchen preparing breakfast – or perhaps he'd never left. Good grief. That was a stupid thing to say. Snap out of it, I told myself. Still, my imagination kept busy creating unwanted, unpleasant visions of Troy and Hannah together. When he finally came to our bed last night, he didn't say a word. He rolled over and went to sleep. That was fine with me. After all, what could he say? "Hi, hon. I've just been making out with your best friend, Hannah?"

What is the matter with me? There, I said it again. Were the three — or was it four? — glasses of wine I drank last night still affecting my intelligence? I had never been in love before, so I wasn't really sure what to do. I had only two choices. Let it go or ask him about the embrace with Hannah. And I was about to do the latter when Trace walked in.

"Mornin', Ivy, Troy. Sleep well?"

"Better than ever," Troy said. "I hope you're up for a big breakfast because one is about to be served."

He asked me to find Kitchi and let him know it was time to eat. Then, he asked Trace if Hannah would be joining us for breakfast. What an odd question. His answer was even stranger.

"I'll check with her. She had a rough night; several nightmares. One way or another, I will be right back."

Oh, dear. Trace looked tired, and he wasn't grinning. No hint of a smile either—all because Hannah had a bad dream? I wondered if they'd argued or had a disagreement.

Kitchi, Troy, and I had begun to eat without them. Kitchi rushed through breakfast, taking just a few bites, said goodbye, and left because he had "things to do." Trace returned soon after that.

"Where's Hannah?" I asked.

"Said she had a late-night snack and wasn't very hungry but asked me to bring her some toast and tea."

A late-night snack, huh? That's not what I'd call it.

"Oh, she also wanted me to tell you that she'd be ready to continue walking and charting the property as soon as we were set to go."

She's stalling because she doesn't want to look me in the eye.

CHAPTER NINE

HANNAH

*E*xcept for the fact that Ivy wouldn't talk to me, the four of us made good progress walking and charting the property. When I realized just how huge it was, it became evident that most of our land would be left wild and natural – a thrilling thought. We'd need less than one-third of it for our current plans. We had a sufficient buffer between our ranch property and, well, more wild and natural land.

At the end of the day, I still hadn't figured out what Ivy's problem was. She acted as if she were mad at me. It's true. I feel weak and out of sorts now and then, which sometimes brings on a spell of nausea. When that happens, I'm not at my best. Not perky, not smiley, and not talkative. But it never lasts very long, and that is not an acceptable reason for her to be angry with me. Perhaps she is the one that feels ill today. I'll do my best to be nice to her, but she's got to meet me halfway and tell me what's wrong.

After dinner, when Troy began to clear the table, I offered to help wash the dishes.

"Sure, Hannah. I never turn down dish-washing help."

"While you two are on kitchen duty, I'll make sure all is well outside," Trace said. "Thought I'd give Beauty a handful of oats. Want Tracker to have some?"

"Sure," Troy said. "Check their blankets too. Okay?"

"Mind if I tag along?" Ivy asked. "I could use a little chilly night air."

I swear Ivy had a smirk on her face when she said that.

"Let's bring the dogs too," Trace added.

"No, I'll take them out later," Ivy said. "Billy, stay here with Troy."

I couldn't believe what was happening. It felt as if Ivy wanted to focus all her attention on Trace and not be bothered watching the dogs or her little boy. And, she wanted me to know that. I couldn't watch the two of them walk out together, so I focused on the dirty dishes. Billy sat at the table drawing pictures.

Standing side by side at the sink, I whispered, "Troy, does Ivy seem okay to you?"

I could tell he was thinking about his reply. His answer was slow in coming.

"Now that you mention it, she's acting out of character, withdrawn, and, at the same time, almost angry."

"Then, it's not just me. I've noticed the same thing. What's causing such a personality change in her?"

"I don't know, but if she keeps it up much longer, I'm going to ask her what's going on."

"Good idea. I'll stay out of it for now, but I am concerned."

I did feel better knowing I was not the only person she expressed anger toward.

"Dad," Billy said. "Can I go sit by the fire with the dogs?"

"Sure, buddy. They'd like that."

We had only two heavy cast iron pots left to clean. Troy took charge of those as I stood ready to dry them. One of the pots was bigger than the sink, so he had to balance it half in the sink and half on the edge of the counter. The pot filled with soapy, greasy water slipped and splashed that water all over both of us before hitting my foot and the floor.

"Damn, that hurts!"

"I'm so sorry. What hurts?" Troy asked.

I didn't know which felt worse—my eye stinging from the soap and grease that splashed into it or my foot throbbing from the pot landing on it.

I couldn't speak yet but patted my eye and limped toward a chair. Troy was quick to assist me. He took off my shoe and applied an ice pack that he grabbed from the freezer after helping me to the chair. Then, he held my face with one hand and dabbed at my eye with the damp, clean cloth he had over his shoulder while we did the dishes.

"Try to stand. See if your foot can endure some weight."

He helped me up. "It hurts, but I can do it."

"Good, now let me take a better look at your eye."

We stood close together, facing each other. Troy placed both hands on my face and tipped my head back and toward the light. "It's definitely red and—"

"I knew it!" Ivy yelled as she barged into the kitchen. "You both have a lot of nerve."

With one eye, I saw her glare at me and maybe even at Troy. Then she turned and stomped out, shoving Trace, who stood in the kitchen doorway, out of her path.

I think we were all stunned by Ivy's anger, especially Troy.

"What the hell just happened?" he asked.

Trace shook his head. "Yeah, I'm wondering about that myself. What's going on in here?"

"Nothing more than washing dishes," I said, limping closer to Trace. "Until that greasy, soap-filled cast iron pot fell on my foot and splashed soap in my eye."

Troy wiped up the spill and rewashed the guilty pot while Trace put his arms around me and asked, "So this is all about a pot?"

I nodded and said, "Pretty much."

Trace helped me sit, looked at my foot, and said, "It's definitely swollen."

"Yes, it is, and I hope nothing is broken." He found the ice pack that had slipped from my foot when I stood. He said nothing more but tenderly placed it back onto my swollen, throbbing injury.

A few moments passed, and still, no one had a good answer for Ivy's odd behavior.

Billy popped his head in the doorway. "Where is mommy going?"

Troy hurried to the living room. Trace and I followed slowly. There, we heard Troy's truck speeding swiftly away. We waited for a reaction from Troy. When none came, Trace tossed his own truck keys to him.

"Go after her."

"Right, but what should I say?"

Trace was quick to answer. "How about, what the hell's going on?"

I did not think Trace's approach would result in an answer from Ivy, let alone an honest one.

"Troy, I think a more caring question might work better," I said. "How about something like this: 'Ivy, please tell me what's bothering you. I'd like to help.' Go on. Try that first. If that fails, use Trace's words."

He dashed from the cabin, and we waited.

Ivy

THERE WAS STILL ice on the windshield of Troy's truck as I sped away. I didn't know where the heat switch or the defroster button was because I'd rarely driven this truck and never in cold, snowy weather. But there was no way I was going to stop right now or even slow down to find and turn on the warmth. Knowing Troy, he'd be following me as soon as it dawned on him that I knew what he had done. I would not let him sweet talk his way out of his improper behavior. Not tonight, not ever. So, I kept driving, speeding.

Other than the truck's headlights, everything ahead of me was dark, pitch black, and blurry. Thinking I was close to the only paved road in the area, I slowed slightly.

Even so, I must have missed it. Soon, there was no road of any kind in sight. And now, I sped forward, looking for a place to turn around. None came, and I began to feel foolish and afraid.

Hannah

WE WERE LYING on top of the covers when midnight had come and gone, and there was still no word from Troy or Ivy. But Trace had a few eye-opening words for me.

"You know, darlin', when Ivy and I came back inside, Troy appeared to be holding you in his arms. At first, that was a troubling sight even for me."

"Oh, Trace. I'm so sorry my injury issue looked suspicious. Thank you for not jumping to a wrong conclusion like Ivy did."

With his fingers, he gently brushed my hair away from my face. "Your eye still looks sore. Did we bring any eye drops?"

"I don't think so, but my eye will be fine in the morning. Not as sure about my foot, though. Trace, right now I'm worried sick. I'm going to call Ivy's cell phone. Why don't you try Troy's?"

Neither picked up, and that surprised me. They must have known how worried we'd be. Trace and I brainstormed every possible reason for them to be gone so long with zero communication. I prayed they were okay and at least communicating with each other.

"I was just thinking that we have no transportation, and I don't feel good about that. What if we had an emergency?"

In a way, I wanted to go down that worrisome path with Trace, but I chose another route.

"In case of an emergency, you will mount Beauty and ride like the wind."

Trace wrapped me in his arms and kissed my neck. "If they are not back by daybreak, I just might do that. In the meantime . . . we're just going to snuggle, cozy up, and hope for a few hours of sleep. What do you say?"

"I say, I love you, Trace McAllister, with all my heart, and I'll be on the back of that horse with you."

Trace got out of bed, took my hand, and led me down the hall, the wrong hall.

"Where are we going?"

"To the room next to Billy's. We'll leave both doors open and the hall light on in case he needs us. If something unforeseen occurs and Troy or Ivy need our help, we'll listen for that too."

"I don't know about you, but there is no way I will participate in a search and rescue operation wearing jammies, so we'd better keep our clothes on." Thinking ahead with my usual practicality, I actually meant that.

Trace grinned, picked me up in his arms, and said, "Let the fully clothed snuggling begin."

I FELT a gentle tapping on my arm and dog breath near my face. The whole crew – Billy, Shadow, Oatie, and Little Charlie – stood by the bed staring at me in the dim light of dawn.

"I can't find Mommy or Daddy. Did they go home without me?"

My tapping on Trace's arm was anything but gentle. He bolted upright.

"They're not back yet?" Trace asked.

I shook my head and then turned my attention to Billy. "No, Billy. They would not leave without you. I'm sure they'll be back soon."

"Promise? Do you promise?"

"Let's you and I whip up an early breakfast," I said. "If I put the ingredients for pancakes into a bowl, would you help me stir it?"

"Yes. I love pancakes. My daddy loves them too. Could we save some for him?"

"Of course, sweetie."

I helped him get dressed so he'd be ready for whatever might take place beyond cooking and eating pancakes.

Standing in the kitchen's archway, I saw Trace build up the fire in the woodstove and then walk out the door with the dogs close behind him. "Going to take my phone with me," he said.

I nodded and began searching for pancake makings. My thoughts, however, were on Troy and Ivy and all the possible reasons for their absence. Had they stopped somewhere to talk and ended up spending the night in a warm, cozy country motel? Or maybe he hadn't found her yet, or there was an accident, or . . . Stop it! Just stop thinking and make pancakes.

Just as I set a plate of perfect pancakes on the table, Trace walked into the kitchen.

"Something smells mighty good in here," he said cheerfully, but his face held a different message. His subtle headshake told me there was still no sign of Troy or Ivy.

For the first time, only three people sat at this huge table, and that felt odd, wrong. The dogs lay quietly nearby, ignoring the food just several feet from their sensitive noses. Billy was the only one behaving in a somewhat normal manner.

"Do you put syrup or sugar on your pancakes, Uncle Trace?"

"I like a little butter and syrup on mine."

"We have *real* syrup, and it is so good. Did you know that some people like fake syrup?"

"No. That's news to me. Sure glad we have the real thing."

As we dug in, the only sounds came from our forks as they clinked against our plates. The stillness bothered me. But then, we heard a subtle sound from outside that got the dogs' attention, and they went dashing from the kitchen barking ferociously.

Trace jumped up and grabbed the gun that he'd placed on top of the fridge when he'd come in for breakfast. He glanced at Billy and me, put a finger to his lips, and said, "Stay here."

CHAPTER TEN

IVY

"We're back," I shouted as I jumped from the truck. Trace opened the cabin's front door, and the dogs bounded straight toward me with such enthusiasm, they almost knocked me down. I wondered if Hannah would be this happy to see me.

"Hey, Troy. I see you've both returned in my truck, but where is yours?" Trace asked.

"Explain our interesting evening, Troy. I've got to go in and talk to Hannah."

"I'll give it a try."

"Hannah? Billy? Where are you?" I said as I walked through the front door. I headed to the kitchen first and arrived before either of them answered. I was surprised to see Hannah sitting in the far corner of the room, holding Billy on her lap.

"Mommy! You're back." He ran to me, and I gave him a huge bear hug.

"Everything is fine, Billy, but could you do me a big favor?" I said.

Wide-eyed and smiling, he nodded.

"Go out and spend a little time with Daddy and the dogs. I'll be there in a few minutes."

He ran out, as I knew he would. Then, I walked toward Hannah wanting to give her a hug, but she shied away. Words would have to do for a while.

"I am so sorry," I said. "I felt physically off-balance, as if I were in someone else's body. That's no excuse for how I behaved, though. I learned last night that I was completely wrong about everything."

"Like what?" Hannah asked hesitantly.

"I saw you and Troy in an embrace one night. And then the next morning you didn't come to breakfast, and we didn't speak during our project work. That night I caught him holding your face and looking sweetly into your eyes. I put two and two together and, unfortunately, came up with an incorrect answer. I just couldn't bear the thought of you and Troy having a romantic relationship."

"So you left?"

"Yes, without thinking, I left. Luckily, Troy tried to

find me. That was tricky for him because I'd ended up at that horrible old cabin five miles south of the main road."

"The cabin our men thought was the final destination for the winter challenge? The one their dad had set up?"

I nodded. "According to Troy, he was too far behind me and didn't see me cross the paved road and continue on the rough and rugged snowy, dirt road, so he headed toward Casper."

"So, how did he find you? And where is his truck?"

"I'd prefer that Troy and I tell the rest of the story together. It is suitable even for young ears."

"Okay. Sure. And, by the way, I do forgive you."

We hugged, and – against my will – a few tears fell from my eyes, proof that my body was still out of sorts.

Hannah said, "Let's join the rest of our group. It sounds like they're in the living room."

I quickly wiped my eyes and put on a happy face.

WE WERE all seated in the living room, staring at the flames flickering through the glass window of the wood-stove. I was expected to tell the story of our disappearance with Troy's help. Awkward was the word of the moment, at least for me. I glanced from person to person until Billy hopped up and sat on my lap.

"Dad said you're going to tell a story."

"Yes, and he's going to help me tell it."

Realizing that I'd spoken too soon about the details being suitable for young ears, I hoped Troy had the same realization. Oh, well. Here goes . . .

"Troy and I had a major misunderstanding, though it was mostly my fault. No, it was all my fault. I needed to get away from Troy and . . . uh, have some space, so there'd be no witnesses to my stupid behavior."

Troy moved over, placed Billy on his lap, and sat beside me. "I think you're being too hard on yourself, babe."

I continued and explained how I'd gone straight across the two-lane paved highway and sped down the rocky, dirt road still covered in places with snow. "It was dark, and I was driving too fast. A creepy, rundown old cabin suddenly came into view when I'd switched on the truck's high beams."

Troy patted my thigh and began to speak. "I didn't actually see what happened next, but I saw the aftermath, and my heart nearly stopped beating."

"I don't know what I'd have done if he hadn't come along." I looked at my man, the love of my life.

"My truck was sideways, nearly upside down, partially covered by a drifted mound of snow. Ivy was still inside, trapped and twisted up in the seatbelt."

"I didn't think I was injured, but I was scared to

death, especially when I heard a vehicle coming toward me and the wrecked truck."

Trace wore a frown and scratched his hatless head. "I'm still unsure of how you found Ivy. Did you see her heading down that dirt road?"

"Nope. I was a little too far behind her, and it never occurred to me that she'd go that way."

"That was unintentional. I didn't mean to go that way," I said.

"Yeah, so how did Troy find you?"

Troy chuckled and looked at Ivy. "I was driving so damn fast once I hit the paved road, I knew I should have caught up with her. Since there had been no other side road to turn off onto, I turned around and headed to the only other road she could possibly have taken. And you know the rest."

Hannah spoke up. "No, not really. Your truck was sideways in a snowdrift, and you were both gone for almost ten hours. We were worried sick."

"Okay, well, your truck had a shovel in the back, and I started digging. I was able to get the truck's door open and untangle Ivy. The old cabin was close by, so we went there to warm up and make sure Ivy wasn't injured."

I knew that cell service around here was iffy, and there was none at all at the old abandoned cabin. So, calling was not an option. I could see that Hannah had a question.

"Why didn't you both get in our truck and drive back here last night?"

I looked at Troy, wondering why we didn't do that.

"Ivy couldn't stop shivering, so I lit a fire in the funky old fireplace in that barely standing old cabin. You know the one. We were all there, briefly, just before Christmas."

"We snuggled up on an uncomfortable couch until the sun came up," I added.

"I'd heard rumors about how great make-up, uh, snuggling could be." Troy winked. "And I can vouch for its greatness."

I glared at Troy, then playfully punched his arm. "Back to reality, my love. Don't forget to call a tow truck.

MOMMA BEAR, DUST BUNNIES, & GUN-TOTING WOMEN

CHAPTER ELEVEN

IVY

Springtime in Montana didn't coincide with the calendar's date for spring. Still, it was worth the wait. By the end of April, the ground had softened, plants had begun to sprout, and I thought I saw some tiny buds on a few of the deciduous trees, although that could have been wishful thinking.

I didn't see Kitchi as often over the past six weeks due to his second job as head contractor of our Wyoming ranch project. We could cover for him because Troy and Saige had stopped scheduling additional guests at our ranch after construction began in Wyoming. He returned once a week for a couple of days to plan and prepare some of the meals for the coming week. He assured Troy this arrangement was not a problem because only a handful of guests and our little family – Cody, Saige, Charlotte, and two wranglers – were there to eat. Troy, Billy, and I dined at home.

Fortunately, no one was fussy about what they ate and were happy to help themselves during the day. Troy and I made sure the shelves, the fridge, and the freezer were well stocked with the basics, and we prepared and served dinner on the nights Kitchi was in Wyoming. Troy loved to cook, and he was an excellent chef. I was fast becoming a talented hostess and waitress.

Troy gave Cody, Willy, and Josh an added bonus for being the clean-up crew in the ranch's huge kitchen and dining hall. With almost no trail rides going out, feeding the horses and mucking the stalls were their only wrangler duties, so they had the time. It wouldn't be long before more guests were scheduled to arrive, and Kitchi would need to be here more often. But he'd planned for that by putting together a construction crew of people he knew and trusted.

My thoughts took a pleasant turn when Billy entered the room.

"Mom, I want to do something fun."

"Okay. Let's go see if Daddy will have time today to take us on a short trail ride."

"Really? I get to ride a horse?"

"I think so, but you'll be riding with either Daddy or me. Okay?"

"Sure! When will I get to ride my own horse?"

I didn't have an answer for him. We'd become over-protective foster parents ever since that couple in the woods tried to steal him from us. I assumed Ms. Cheryl, Billy's caseworker, hadn't gotten wind of the attempted kidnapping since we hadn't heard from her. Come to think of it, we hadn't heard from law enforcement either. I made a mental note to ask Troy about that.

Some days, I wished Troy and I would just run away and elope. The sooner we were married, the sooner the official adoption could take place, and we wouldn't have to worry about anyone taking Billy away from us. At least not legally.

"We'll see what Troy thinks about you riding on your own horse. Maybe this summer."

He jumped up and down with joy the entire walk to Troy's office. This kid was delightful and happy almost all the time. And that rubbed off on us.

Troy sat with his back to us as we approached the open door to his macho, rustic office, the place where we'd first met. Back then, I was a new guest at the ranch and had been snooping around looking for the treasure I'd heard about. That first meeting was a dreadful disaster but look at us now.

Troy was on a call in speakerphone mode. I put my finger to my lips to let Billy know we should be quiet and not disturb him until the call was over. We'd wait patiently inside the lodge just a few feet from his office door.

"So we are still being harassed by some unknown entity?" I heard Troy say.

"Very minor stuff, but yes, you, me, or the property itself is on someone's let's-make-trouble list." I recognized the sound of Kitchi's voice.

"What's our next move with regard to the *trouble*?"

"I'm headed back to Montana tomorrow, but I've got a crew of six talented men that will remain and keep working. They are looking forward to handling any additional trouble, should it show up."

"Hurry back. You're missed here."

"Inform Ivy that construction is ahead of schedule. The women's little chapel is almost complete."

"Will do," Troy confirmed and then ended the call.

I forgot about being silent and did some of my own noisy jumping for joy. Troy turned in surprise. "Hey, there," he said and then paused. "How much of our conversation did you hear?"

Billy ran up to his daddy. "Lots! Cause we were being silent."

Oh, dear. Out of the mouths of babes again. "Just a little. A sentence or two," I said.

"Well, there's been a little trouble, but Kitchi assures me it's very minor – probably done by a teenager – and the crew will take care of it. Not to worry."

"Good! And, the old, charred barn is almost ready? Hannah and I should finalize some of the interior décor. Could you ask Kitchi to send photos today since he's leaving tomorrow?"

"Huh. I guess you heard more than a couple of sentences. Get over here, Ivy."

Troy's face carried a serious, no-nonsense expression. I held my breath.

"I want to kiss you," he said, winking.

Breathing and smiling once again, I stepped closer, ready for his lips on mine. Mmm. A delicious kiss that would have gone on far longer had Billy not said, "Hey, we're here to ride horses."

With raised eyebrows, Troy glanced up at me. "You are?"

"Yes, kind of. We planned to ask if you would take us on a short trail ride."

"I think we can do that. Let me call Kitchi back first. I'll meet you at the house for a quick lunch, then we'll ride. Sound good?"

We were already heading out the door.

. . .

BILLY RODE with me on Tracker, and Shadow rode with Troy on Gunner. Yes, Troy, the cowboy who wanted nothing to do with pets, held our coyote pup with one arm and the reins with the other. If only someone had been nearby to snap a photo of this unusual foursome. I'd love to have this sweet moment reproduced and hung on our wall.

The sound of the horses' hooves plodding on the ground and the easy rocking motion we felt as they moved along almost lulled Billy and me into a dream-like state of mind. Mixed with the hush offered by the surrounding pines and low junipers, I felt more at ease than I had in a long time. The loud chirp of a pair of Cardinals caught our attention.

"I like those red birds," Billy said.

"Me too," I replied.

"Let's take a short break," Troy suggested. "This looks like a good spot. Plenty of room for the horses, complete with a couple of perfect tree limbs that I'll hook their long lead ropes to."

Troy dismounted first, set Shadow down, and then reached up for Billy. I didn't need assistance with my dismount, but once my feet hit the ground, oh, boy, my knees gave out. When Troy offered me a hand, I took it.

Within minutes I regained the use of my legs. All was well.

"Anybody thirsty? I've got water or soda. What do you want, Billy?"

"What are you having, Dad?"

"For now, water."

"Then that's what I want too."

Most people sit when taking a break. Not us. Our legs, mostly mine, needed stretching, so we stood a bit, and we walked around some, although we remained in the small clearing. I kept watch over Billy as he explored the edges of the clearing, and Troy kept his eye on Shadow except when he went over to the horses to retrieve our drinks. That's when our pup spotted a squirrel.

"Shadow!" I called. I could hear her thrashing in the bushes. "Shadow?" I repeated. Billy called her too. I wasn't worried knowing she was nearby, but I wondered if she'd catch that squirrel and hoped she wouldn't. "Troy, our pup needs to attend dog training school. For her own safety, she must come when we call her."

"We'll work on that, but not—" Suddenly, the forest was no longer quiet or peaceful. Shadow howled, squirrels screeched, and the horses stomped and squealed. "They're spooked. That's odd," he said, looking around for the cause. He grabbed his gun instead of the water.

I saw Billy run toward the bushes where a tiny bear had emerged. "It's a baby. It needs our help," he said, showing no fear.

"No, Billy. No!" Everything happened so fast.

I ran toward him and pushed him behind me just as help arrived. Not for me, not for our boy, but for the cub. Troy was a few seconds too late for me but shouted to Billy. "Go stand between the two horses. Now!"

I froze, certain that running wasn't a good strategy. The next thing I knew, Shadow was at my feet, howling and showing her tiny teeth, her way of telling the bear to get lost. Pretty sure that strategy wouldn't work either.

Positioned in front of her cub, the mother bear swiped, grazing me with her paw just as Troy shot his gun in the air above the bear's head. Then, the medium-sized black bear stood tall, huffing and snorting, warning us to stay far away from her and her cub. I'd gladly do that.

Once the two bears were out of sight, I felt the sting on my face and saw the blood on my hand. With his arm around my waist, Troy walked me back to the horses. First, he set Billy up on Gunner and then tended to my injury. The pup never left my side, but I could see her small body shaking. We were lucky. We all survived, and I felt no anger toward the bear. She was just protecting her cub. I could relate to that.

Troy took a cloth from his saddlebag as well as one of the bottles of water he'd brought for us to drink. "You're going to have a scar," he said as he dabbed the cut with the wet cloth.

"I don't care," I said, surprising myself and wondering if I might be in shock.

"You're beautiful, even with this new badge of bravery."

Then I remembered that Troy had facial scars too from last October's plane crash. We'd be the scar-faced twins.

"If someday you do care, we can call that plastic surgeon that gave me his card when we were in the hospital. Maybe we'll be awarded a two-for-one surgical deal."

It seemed Troy recalled that same memory. "I think you threw his card in the trash," I teased.

He helped me mount Tracker, then handed me a clean, dry cloth that I held to my face to slow the bleeding. My body trembled, and I had to admit that I felt shaken. Never had a bear smack me before. Troy handed Shadow to Billy while he mounted Gunner, then he reached around for the pup.

"I can hold Shadow," Billy said, sounding strong and hopeful.

"I know you can, little buddy. I want you to hold my belt with both hands. That's important right now."

"Okay." His disappointment was obvious.

Troy grabbed the reins attached to my horse, made a quick *click-click* sound to get the horses moving, and led us back to the ranch. At first, I was insulted; I was a decent rider now. So, I shot back one of his often-used phrases. "I got this."

"Humor me, babe. You need one hand to hold the cloth to your face and the other to grab the saddle horn if necessary. I've got Billy and the pup. We're all going to be fine."

"Fine." I said with a pout. I should appreciate that he's looking out for me and being caring. Even though he was right, he made me feel like a child.

"And you can keep an eye on all three of us from back there."

We hadn't gone far when Troy took out his SAT phone. All I heard him say was, "See if Dr. Mick can meet us at the ranch in about 30 minutes. We have an emergency." Then, he turned his head toward me and asked, "When was your last tetanus shot, Ivy?"

I gasped. "Not sure." A needle was not my friend. Okay for others, but not for me. Troy would soon see another one of my flaws up close and personal.

. . .

A FEW WEEKS had passed since our meet-up with the bear. I came through the tetanus shot with flying colors, but now the scabs on my cheek were tight and sore even though the five stitches had been removed. Some days I was grumpy and blamed that on the bear.

Troy acted as if the bear encounter – that's what he called it – was all his fault no matter how many times I assured him it wasn't. It was just one of those nature things. A momma bear doing her job. Billy couldn't get enough of hearing the bear encounter story, and he thought I was the bravest mother in the whole world. I could live with that.

In no mood to talk on the phone, I sent a text to Hannah letting her know that Kitchi had been arranging a work of art for the chapel in Wyoming for some time. Two horses had been included in the stained glass design. Kitchi showed me a picture, and the art looked magnificent.

Hannah returned my text saying she was excited to see the stained glass and had lots of comments about her vision for the chapel's interior. For some reason, I was almost instantly aggravated. I wanted to keep the interior simple. Additional décor should be brought in after we'd spent more time there. I wasn't ready to reply, knowing I had nothing positive to say, so I turned off my phone. For now, in my opinion, the chapel just had to accommodate the few people we'd invite to our double wedding.

I heard the front door open. "Troy?"

"Yes, ma'am. In person. Are you busy right now?" he asked, walking into the living room, where I had been sitting.

"Just texting Hannah, that's all."

"Do you and Billy want some lunch? I'm cooking if you do."

"Maybe in a little while." I might be having one of my grumpy bear days. "Hannah thinks Kitchi should add several shelves to the one windowless wall and some movable pew-like benches in the chapel," I told Troy. "Can you believe that?"

"Yeah, that sounds good."

"Well, all of a sudden, she's got a bunch of ideas, and I don't like any of them."

"Why? Does it really matter?"

I shook my head. No, it didn't matter, and I didn't know why I pretended it did. Another wave of feeling a little out of sorts, off-balance, had come over me.

"Ivy, enough already. You're starting to act like a woman with PMS and—"

I wagged my finger at him and felt my anger growing. "Don't you dare go there. You know about my physical limitation. I can't possibly have that syndrome."

"I'm so sorry. It's just that I'm worried about you and these mood swings. It's not like you."

He took me in his arms, and calmness swept over me. He was right. I didn't like myself when I acted so weird . . . and just plain awful.

"Hey, babe. Let's do something special. Just you and me."

"All right. What did you have in mind?"

"I'm taking you away from working The Lonely Horse Ranch and stressing over your new ranch for the rest of the day. We are going to the waterfall for a little R and R."

We'd only been there one other time. I was happy to be going back again despite the bear encounter we'd had last time. What is it with bears and me? Troy took Billy and Shadow over to spend a couple hours with Saige, and then he put together some snacks and drinks. I gathered a couple of blankets, and off we went, this time via a quad rather than horseback.

Nothing disrupted the romance this time. The closest thing to a bear encounter was me. I was nearly bare. And now, right here in broad daylight, it was hard to miss the fact that I'd gained a few pounds. Maybe that's the problem, the reason for my mood swings. I'd always been in great shape. "Do I look heavier to you, Troy?"

"Oh, I'm definitely not going there, babe. And I can't

believe these words are coming from your beautiful mouth."

"Ever since Billy was almost kidnapped, I've been hovering over him. I haven't used your state-of-the-art gym like I did in the past. I haven't even been in the big barn that houses it."

"Let's fix that. What if we added a kid's activity center in one of the corners just for Billy? He could go with you or me and play while we work out. Problem solved."

CHAPTER TWELVE

HANNAH

*I*t was the week of the Memorial Day holiday, and I would have extra time on my hands. Trace had two out-of-town meetings: One with a Spanish Barb organization and the other with the BLM to look over some wild mustang stock. He'd return the evening of the third day. He invited me to come along, and I was tempted, but I detected hesitation in his offer.

That was all right because, in my mind, I was already filling up the time I'd gain in his absence. I'd visit Rosa at The Big Mack, paint a portrait of Trace with Blackjack – I had the perfect photo to work from – and spend more time with my horses, dogs, and cows. Yes, even the cows.

We didn't sleep much the night before he left. We

made love with the desperation of a couple being separated due to a military assignment in a foreign land even though we'd only be apart for three days and two nights.

I stood outside in the dark, watching Trace put his duffle bag, snacks, and camera into the truck. He'd have a busy three days, and so would I. The time had come for him to go. He wrapped his arms around my shivering body.

"I'm not good with leaving you here. Memories of the day you were kidnapped are carved into my brain and my heart and—"

"I know. That was an awful time, but I have my own gun now. And the bad guys are no longer alive."

The only hassle I might receive would come from Callie, the nineteen-year-old woman who'd wanted Trace all to herself for eternity. She'd made it perfectly clear last summer, shortly after I arrived, that she wanted me gone. Can't shoot her for speaking mean and hurtful words, though I'd be pleased to never see her again. That gal was persistent.

Trace had insisted I learn to shoot – and to shoot well. He was a wonderful teacher, and I became a darn good shot if I do say so myself.

"But you have to carry your gun all the time if it's going to keep you safe. Hold on a second." He stepped to the back of his truck and rummaged through the huge toolbox in the truck bed. "Here you go," he said, easing into a smile as he handed me a small holster. "I feel better now that you can carry your gun at all times until I return."

After one last luscious kiss, he was gone. I went back to bed for a couple of hours; Oatie and Little Charlie were quick to join me.

THE SUN SHONE brightly this beautiful morning, warming the ground and filling the air with the scent of new growth. I used to dread the coming of summer when I lived in Phoenix and the temperature would hover over one hundred degrees for at least three months. Here, I looked forward to the pleasant warmth of summer.

Trace had pulled out before the sun was up, and I missed him already. The dogs and I walked the length of our 400-foot gravel driveway to check the mailbox. Well, I walked; the dogs bounded, frolicked, and ran circles around me. I hadn't checked the mailbox for a couple days. No big deal; we rarely received anything interesting, though occasionally there was a catalog or two.

To my surprise, we got mail! Not just bills this time. One envelope looked like a personal letter addressed to The McAllisters.

"Should I open it?" I asked the dogs. I was not officially a McAllister yet, so I carried all the mail back to the house and set it on the kitchen counter with the letter on top. I let it sit there for two whole days, although I glanced at that envelope many times.

Oh, heck, I couldn't look at it lying there anymore and decided to open it. It was short but not sweet. All it said was, *Mr. McAllister, Your money or your life.* I stared at the ominous words and, after reading them many times over, a revelation came to me. The cryptic note had a total of seven words. Seven! But seven was our lucky number. How could this be? Was it a coincidence? A mere joke? Nothing about the words was funny. Or was it written by someone taking advantage of our frightening recent past? But who would do that? And why?

Better late than never, I hurried to the bedroom and retrieved my gun from its bedside location. Then, with just the right amount of daring, I slipped it into the holster and buckled up. The dogs watched the entire procedure and seemed to await my next move. Heck. I was wondering about my next move too. Should I try to call Trace? Yes. I pressed his cell number on The Lucky Seven's landline and waited. The call did not go through. That's what I was afraid of. He's out of cell range. I could call Sheriff Jane or Ivy? Jane was the closest. Yes, I should let her know.

I called and was placed on hold, then, "Sheriff speaking."

"Hi, Jane. This is Hannah from The Lucky Seven."

"Hey, what's going on? You've never called me before."

"Trace is out of town. He won't be back until tomorrow." I knew I was talking too fast and making myself out of breath.

"Okay. Slow down and tell me what's wrong."

"I went to the mailbox to get our mail. There was a letter, and it sounded threatening, and I don't know what to do about it."

"Did it threaten you?"

I wasn't sure how to answer that. I wasn't a McAllister yet. "No, not me directly, just Trace."

"What did the letter say?"

"It said, Your money or your life."

"I see." Jane paused. "If you're sure Trace will be back tomorrow, you'll be fine. It's likely just a prank anyway, but keep your doors locked, and feel free to call me anytime. I will answer your call 24/7 until Trace returns."

"Thank you. I feel so much better after speaking with you."

"Any time, Hannah. Any time."

I breathed normally once again and went back to the

kitchen feeling a bit like a gunslinger. A vision of Annie Oakley — or was it Calamity Jane? (I get my gun-toting western women confused sometimes) – brought a hint of an ever so brief giggle to my lips.

Of course, I wouldn't shoot the mail carrier, but I could shoot up the letter. No, we might need it for evidence someday. What was I to do? This was a threat! Intimidation, but not from Callie; this wasn't her style. She would not want to hurt Trace. Me, maybe, but not Trace. Good grief. I'm talking to myself far too much today. I needed a human, preferably the man I love.

I jerked, hearing the landline ring. Was it Jane calling back? Maybe it was Trace. Either way, the sound distracted me from my rambling thoughts.

"Hannah? It's Ivy. I've got some fantastic news."

"Great! I could use some good news, but I need to ask you a question first."

"Okay, shoot."

If she only knew how ironic her two little words were. "Could you ask Troy if anything unusual has occurred recently? Strange mail, phone calls, things out of place?" I asked.

"That is an odd question, Hannah. Has something happened?"

"Just a short, creepy note. It's probably nothing, just a prank."

"Sure, I'll ask him, though I'm certain he would have told me of any such trouble. I'm surprised you didn't call him directly to ask your question," Ivy said.

There was something off about her tone, but I let it go for now because I didn't want to think about that note anymore. "I want to hear all about the good news."

"Kitchi called from our Wyoming ranch last night to let us know that his crew had finished the charred barn remodel. They've already broken ground on the bunkhouse and have requested any input we might have about that structure."

"Did he send any drawings or dimensions?" I asked.

"He did. I'll upload them to you after we hang up. Be sure to share them with Trace."

"He's been out of town for a couple days, but I'll—"

"Do I detect a little trouble in paradise?"

"No! Why would you say that?" Two odd comments in one brief phone call. What is messing with Ivy's mind today? Or am I too sensitive and reading too much into her words? Recently, though, it did seem she had a snippy attitude a little too often.

"I'll send you my thoughts about the interior of our chapel after I take a look at what's already been done. You can share those with Kitchi and, of course, Troy." Now I had an attitude. Snippiness must be contagious.

I'd already sent a few thoughts earlier, but I looked forward to seeing a recent version of the finished chapel.

DAY THREE HAD ARRIVED, and tonight so would Trace. Staring into the freezer and the pantry for the makings of a romantic dinner, it seemed a trip to town was necessary to pull that off. I'd better hurry; the nearest grocery store was thirty miles away.

Halfway down the driveway, my phone trilled with an incoming text message. I stopped the Jeep and looked at the screen. The message was from Trace. *Hi darlin'. I'll be gone one extra day and out of cell and Internet range for part of that day. Didn't want you to worry. Love you. Miss you. See you tomorrow.* I missed him too, but I'd be fine. I had my animals, my holstered gun on my hip, and lots of photos of the chapel to look at and comment on. I'd be so busy that the extra day would fly by.

TRACE'S RETURN brought The Lucky Seven back to normal. The dogs couldn't get enough of him; neither could I. After one, long delicious kiss from my man, he took my hand, and we all walked outside.

"Humor me, darlin', I just need to walk around our

little ranch, see the animals, and stretch my legs. I've been sitting in my truck for too many hours."

The dogs followed along as we checked on the chickens, gave my two horses some treats, and, to my delight, walked to the lower pasture where my four cows grazed. Now, instead of being tired from sitting in his truck, Trace seemed wired with newfound energy from walking up and down the hilly pasture.

"Let's head back to the house," he said. I saw no grin on his face when he spoke those words, so I knew he had no ulterior motive, but that was odd because we hadn't been together for several days.

Back at the house, I kept busy putting some details on my recent drawing. Through the window, I could see Trace leaning against the deck railing, looking at his cell phone. "Hannah, a text from Troy just popped up. Can you join me out here? I think you're going to want to see this."

If a voice could smile, Trace's was grinning from ear to ear. "Be right there," I said as I put down my drawing pencil and anticipated some good news. Trace held up his phone as I walked toward him. All I saw was four little words: THE CHAPEL IS DONE! "The chapel is done? Really? That is super great news," I said. Should I tell him I already knew that?

"And I think we should celebrate."

"Yes! For sure." I meant that, though initially, my first thoughts were about the ranch project and what we should tackle next.

"Earth to Hannah. Where did you go? You know I'll give you several pennies for your thoughts."

"Sorry, I got lost in thought for a second. I'm just so happy that it's finished, but now, I think we all deserve a little R and R. Let's go to Wyoming and take an up-close look at the accomplishments of Kitchi and his crew."

"Okay, but I'd like you and me to celebrate today."

"Do you have something specific in mind?" I wondered.

Trace hesitated, so I simply waited. At the moment, I had no ideas to contribute.

"If you don't want to do this, I will understand."

What could he be thinking? He had my full attention.

"I'd like to take a drive and have a champagne toast up at the lake cabin. I guess we should call it something else now that the cabin no longer exists. Will it bother you to see its charred remains still lying there?"

"I won't know until I'm there." I'd seen charred remains before, but that was a very different situation. As long as I didn't see any human bones among those remains, I'd be okay. "I'd love to see the lake again and the small hot springs puddle that saved our lives."

"Then it's settled. If you would feed your horses, I'll get everything ready for our celebration."

I LOVED MY HORSES. Lewissa and I connected the first day we met, though I have to give her all the credit. She showed me how intelligent and humorous she was. I still remember that morning like it was yesterday. I'd walked over to the corral where she and Clark spent much of their time and apologized for being clueless about horses and ranch life.

I spoke to her and said, "I hope you'll forgive my rookie mistakes. You see, I've become both a novice rancher and a fake widow today. How many people can say that, huh?"

The mare blinked, then stomped the ground once with her front hoof, and I shook my head and laughed out loud. We've been good friends ever since. I didn't laugh the horrific day she saved my life and Trace's, though I will always be grateful for her intuition, endurance, and bravery.

I spoil her now; she deserves it. I gave both horses their usual flake of hay and a handful of alfalfa. "You two take care of each other. Trace and I will be gone for the day." I slipped them each a peppermint treat before heading back inside.

"I'm ready if you're ready," Trace said, his arms loaded with blankets and a picnic basket.

"Let's go!"

The ride up the mountain was a bumpy one over rocks, tree branches, and a minor mudslide. I'd wished for a life of adventure a year ago, and oh, boy did I get my wish. I hadn't wished to fall in love, though. But here I was, head over cowboy-boot heels in love with a wonderful, handsome man.

Trace parked his truck facing away from those charred remains. We got out and took the blankets and snacks to the edge of the pristine mountain lake. Before we began our picnic, he took me in arms and said, "You know how much I love you, right?"

I nodded. I knew he cared for me too. Neither of us was perfect, but we were pretty darn close. I'd forgotten how the silence up here seemed almost deafening. It took several minutes for my ears to adjust to being far from the noises of a ranch or a town.

Trace lifted the small, two-serving bottle of champagne from the picnic basket. I wondered if the bumpy ride had created a few extra bubbles in that bottle. I'd soon find out.

The cork popped, making an impressive, festive sound, and flew through the air as champagne flowed down Trace's arm. He poured what was left of the champagne into two glasses. I remained amazed by his relationship with alcohol. He only drank champagne. Not very much and not very often.

"To us! Today, tomorrow, and forever," he said.

We sipped the tiny servings of the bubbly and engaged in our longest, most passionate kiss to date. If we hadn't needed to breathe, we'd still be kissing.

Trace pulled away, inches only, and asked, "Hungry?"

"As a matter of fact, I am." I stared at the picnic basket that Trace seemed to be guarding. Why would he do that? His last picnic surprise was a buffalo hide. Oh, no. He wouldn't dare bring a buffalo sandwich. He knows I'm a vegetarian.

I watched as he removed a small, portable camp stove from the basket, lit the canister with a match, and placed a covered pot on top. Before long, I could smell the delicious aroma and knew we'd be eating chili.

"You're cooking!" I said, surprised. His brother was the chef in the family. I don't think I've ever seen Trace prepare food.

He grinned and confessed, "No, not cooking. Just heating up some of Rosa's chili that she'd made last night for the wranglers at The Big Mack."

I must have had a concerned look on my face because he added, "Don't worry. It's vegetarian chili. You're going to love it."

Trace also brought two blue metal camp-style bowls and a baguette for dipping into the chili. And dip we did. I loved it. Between the two of us, we ate it all.

"Let's go for a walk around the lake," I said. "I've only been between the cabin and the small hot springs pool."

"We don't have enough time to go all the way around; that's for another day. Still, I think you'll like what you see."

"I'm sure I will."

The air was pristine, the water crystal clear. I was glad we stopped often as the high altitude took my breath away almost as much as Trace did. Hearing a shrill cry high above me, I looked toward the sound coming from the deep blue sky and saw two birds that seemed to be floating. As they circled around, gliding lower and lower, I knew they were huge birds.

"Hawks?" I asked.

"Nope, eagles. Immature eagles. They won't wear their well-known white heads until they're at least five years old."

"So, you're an eagle expert?"

"No, but I've spent time around them, and they've taught me quite a bit. They have the best eyesight in the entire animal world."

"They didn't teach you that."

"You're right. I read about eagles when I attended veterinarian school."

If only I'd brought along my drawing pad and a pencil or two. Come to think of it, next time we go to town, I'd purchase a small sketching pad that I can carry with me everywhere I go. I'll never miss an opportunity like this again.

The eagles swooped so close to us I could hear the whooshing sound from their wings. "Wow! That eagle is huge. Are you sure it's immature?"

"For starters, the female eagles are sometimes larger than the males. And, here's the best part, they mate for life."

He grinned and took my hand. "We'd better head back to the truck."

On the drive down the mountain to The Lucky Seven, I could tell by his face that Trace was deep in thought. I knew that face well. I stroked his cheek with the back of my fingers. "What's up, my one and only?"

He stopped the truck. No need to pull over; we'd meet no other vehicles on this dirt road that went only to this non-working, high-altitude McAllister property. "I'd rather not go to Wyoming for several weeks. I have committed to another educational horse-shopping trip."

"Oh . . . all right." A thoughtful moment passed, and I continued. "When we get back to the house, you can tell me which days you'll be gone, and then I'll call Ivy to check on their schedule. After that, we will set some dates for our R and R as well as the double wedding – the sooner, the better."

KNOWING the dates for Trace's travel commitment, I was ready to call Ivy and set up our next trip to Wyoming. I called her cell phone first and was surprised to hear the sound of Troy's voice. "Hi, did I call the wrong number? This is Hannah, and I'd hoped to speak with Ivy."

"You got the right number; I've got the wrong phone," Troy said with a chuckle.

"I don't understand. You traded phones?"

"Not on purpose. I've got hers, and she's got mine." He laughed, seeming unconcerned.

"Should I call your number?" I wasn't sure I had his number. "When do you expect she'll have her phone back?"

"As soon as she figures out what happened, she'll call me. I have no doubt." He laughed again. Perhaps an inside joke existed between them concerning their phones.

"Okay. Since we're talking, I've got a question for you. Trace and I think it would be nice to take a few days off and drive to the Wyoming property to check out the chapel and the current construction. And include a little R and R too. Are there any days in the near future that you and Ivy cannot do that?"

"Our calendars are free of extra travel except for the Montana Ranchers Association annual meeting the last week in June. We'd just need a little notice to make sure all the activities here at The Lonely Horse Ranch are covered."

"Good. I'll get back to you both with some dates." I was about to end the call when another question came to mind. "Troy, other than the incident with Billy, have you received any additional threats, vandalism, or anything out of the ordinary?"

"Not that I'm—"

"Who are you talking to on *my* phone?" I heard Ivy interrupt, and she wasn't laughing.

"It's Hannah. We were discussing a quick trip to Wyoming. Here. You talk to her."

"I don't feel like talking to anyone right now."

"Well, you better talk to me," Troy said.

Their strong voices were easy to overhear, and their words had an edge I didn't understand. Was Ivy mad at Troy? Was she upset that I was talking to him? Either way, I wasn't up to participating in her irritable mood. Since she didn't want to talk, I quickly hung up and turned off my phone. Still, I worried about her and wondered what was wrong. She's usually so creative, sensible, and strong, but every now and then . . .

At least I'd fulfilled the purpose of my call. Based on Troy's information, I decided on a date for all of us to travel to Wyoming. I'd ask Trace to call them back tomorrow to say that the 4th of July was the day we'd all meet at the Wyoming property.

CHAPTER THIRTEEN

IVY

*I*t was the 4th of July, and Troy, Billy, Shadow, and I arrived at the Wyoming cabin before anyone else. We'd planned it that way, wanting to tidy up the cabin a bit. Kitchi let us know that his crew had headed home for a much-needed break and the holiday, but he doubted they had time to clean up the place before leaving.

Troy lifted up the rusty metal cover of the fuse box and flipped every switch to its On position. With fingers crossed, we stepped inside and turned on some lights. Voila! We had electricity. Scanning the living room, we saw that it wasn't cluttered, but it wasn't clean either. We could handle that. Now, to unload the truck. We'd brought most of the food this time because Troy insisted on cooking all the dinners. We had an ice chest full of food and ingredients and several crates of non-perishables. We carried those inside first.

"I'll organize all the food," I said and began that task right away.

"As soon as I set up the panels for the portable corral, I'll see you back in the kitchen," Troy said.

"Maybe. Maybe not. I bet I'll be done in the kitchen before you return."

Billy and the dogs kept an eye on us as we went back and forth accomplishing our self-assigned tasks. Finally, Billy said, "Just kiss him, Mom, so he'll let the horse out of the trailer."

"Great idea, Billy. I think I will." I followed through and surprised Troy with a kiss on the lips right there on the porch. Then I explained my agenda. "I'll visit the ladies' room next and then check all the bedrooms."

"Yes, ma'am. Sounds like a plan."

My man was in good spirits today. Actually, we both were.

I handed Billy a feather duster and gave him two jobs. Dust the living room, watch Shadow, and keep the front door locked.

"Okay, but that's three jobs, not two," he said.

He was brighter than the average five year old. Heck,

he was more insightful than many people I'd met in my life. "My error. You're absolutely right. Can you handle all that?"

"Of course." He went straight to the front door, turned, and informed me, "It's locked." He then began smacking every surface in the room with the duster. Shadow hid, and I dashed to the ladies' room.

After washing up, I began to check the bedrooms. The beds weren't made, and the sheets hadn't been washed, but there was no way to wash them here. Check the closets, I told myself. Knowing Alice, Troy and Trace's mom, she'd likely brought extra sets of sheets when we were here last December.

And there they were. Already this had become a two voila day. I ripped the used sheets from the bed and replaced them with never-used sheets. The bed-making chore didn't take long because I was feeling good today and worked fast. Next, I headed to the kitchen to check on Troy.

"So you've finished setting up the temporary corral? How are things in here?" I stood in the doorway watching Troy up to his elbows in soapy water.

"Almost. Thought I'd get started on these dirty dishes. It seems that one of the crew knew how to cook. Good thing, 'cause there was no fast food or a single restaurant within an hour's drive."

"I know you like things clean and tidy, but we're only going to be here for a few days, so don't knock yourself out."

"I won't, but I can't live with this thick layer of grease that's covering almost every surface on or near the stove. I'm betting that someone cooked a lot of fry bread and everything else with tons of oil."

I asked Troy how long he'd be in the kitchen this afternoon. He thought he could make it *good enough* and wrap things up within thirty minutes. I went to check on Billy and his dusting project. Sunlight streamed in the living room windows allowing me to see the well-dusted surfaces. The bright light also made the air look as if it were snowing dust particles. I didn't see Billy or Shadow, but I noticed that the front door was still closed. He must be dusting the bedrooms, I thought.

I moved from room to room quietly, hoping to get a peek at the child's dusting technique. When I could not find him, there was no other choice but to call his name.

"Billy? Billy, where are you?" Shadow came running with joyful enthusiasm. Got to love a coyote pup. She tugged at my jeans; her hind end up in the air as if we were playing a game. I went along with it. She took me to the next room. I still didn't see Billy, but I heard giggling. Then Shadow disappeared under the bed. And within seconds, I was on all fours looking under that bed at Billy and the pup.

"Dusting under here is hard. Look, Mom. Balls of dust."

"Come out. We don't need to dust under beds this time."

When Billy and Shadow scooted out on their bellies, they were covered in dust. I walked him to the mirror for a look at himself. All I said was, "Dust bunnies."

"Giant dust bunnies," he added with a little grin on his face.

I took them both outside to brush away the clinging bunnies. That's when we heard Trace's truck pulling in. Troy must have heard it too, or he wanted to be part of the dust bunny removal task. Either way, he stood right beside us.

Hannah got down from the truck and hurried toward me. Oatie and Little Charlie followed at her heels. Within seconds, I received an enthusiastic hug – I'd been so wrong about my suspicions – and the dogs danced around Billy, excited to see him again. The men were far more reserved. Striding toward each other as if this was no big deal. But it was a big deal. We hadn't seen each other for almost four months.

"Let's unload your truck," I said. "I think you will be

pleased with our clean-up project. The crew left a mess, but we took care of most of it."

Troy laughed out loud. "Ivy's right. That's what we did, well, all but the bathrooms. We saved those two little rooms for you to do."

Trace took off his cowboy hat and scratched his head. "I guess we should have driven slower, arrived later." Now everyone laughed.

"Ivy, have you checked our little chapel?" Hannah asked.

"No, we were waiting for you. I want us all to oooh and aaah together," I said with a smile. This was going to be a great day.

Hannah

TRACE HELPED Troy finish setting up the temporary corral. Once it was up, they'd fill a water bucket, toss in a few flakes of hay, and walk the horses over to it. It was in a perfect location, not far from the cabin. Leafy trees provided shade on one side of the round pen, and the sun shone on the other side.

Finally, the time had come. The unveiling of the old barn's transformation from charred to charming—a relaxing, peaceful retreat—was about to take place. Walking toward it, I was delighted that the scent of burnt wood was gone completely. I'd thought it might linger for a while. Instead, a hint of fresh paint greeted my sensitive nose.

"Son of a gun," Trace stated. "Kitchi must have instructed the crew to demolish the entire structure and build the chapel from the ground up."

We all stood, awestruck. The photos were taken so close up that none of us realized that the front double-door was on a different side of the structure than before. A charming rock-lined path led the way to that entrance.

"I wonder what other surprises Kitchi has in store for us," Ivy said, her voice filled with excitement.

Shrugs all around.

Troy held up a key. "Ready. Set. Let's go find out."

Like a parade, including the pets, we all hurried toward the entrance. But then, we stopped quicker than an arrow hitting a brick wall when we heard Troy say, "Uh, we have a problem."

"What's wrong?" Ivy asked from the back of the line.

Troy stepped aside and pointed to the smashed lock on the door.

Trying to be positive, dozens of logical possibilities tumbled through my mind. Maybe someone was in desperate need of shelter. But, if so, why didn't they break into the main cabin? As fast as those possibilities arrived, they were followed by a bunch of *buts*.

Troy, with a gun in hand, was the first one inside. "Damn! Someone's been here."

We crept in cautiously. I gasped at the horrifying sight. Trace shook his head and let out a string of rarely used cuss words. Ivy scooped Billy up in her arms and held him tightly. The dogs stood very still. The sight was grotesque, unbelievable. Who would do such a thing? And for what purpose?

Vandals had spray painted the new chapel's interior with red, white, and blue paint. No design to their artwork, just ugly blotches of paint covering every surface and in every direction. I could feel the anger of ghost-like culprits darting around within these walls.

I'd never seen Ivy so mad. If looks could kill, somebody would be dead by now. Seething with sarcasm, she followed that look with, "At least they were patriotic. Happy July 4th, everyone." She took Billy back outside, and the dogs followed.

The beautiful, handcrafted, stained-glass window with the two horses built into the design had not been spared. I listened to Troy and Trace's exchange of words while I knelt down and gathered up the broken pieces of glass.

"Is anything in here salvageable?" Trace asked.

"Only if we want a red, white, and blue poorly

painted chapel. The vandals had a field day with an axe too." Troy shook his head at the unbelievable sight. "Every wooden shelf, table, chair, and even the riser has been demolished. A wrecking ball could not have done a better job."

"Yeah," Trace said. "Here we go again. Another one step forward and 100 steps back."

Troy began to pace. "Not only were these vandals thorough, but they also worked fast. Kitchi's crew has only been gone a few days."

"But there have been no demands. Who in their right mind would take the time to do all this?" Trace said, "That's the part that makes no sense to me . . . unless their ultimate goal was to make us miserable."

I could no longer remain out of this conversation. "Well, it's working. I'm miserable." So much ugliness. Will this ever end? This was no place for a wedding, not even a small, simple one. Not even if the ceremony was held outdoors.

"I'm going outside to take a look around and see if any clues pop up," Troy said as he headed for the door.

Trace took my hand. "Come on, Hannah. Let's get some fresh air."

"Ivy," Troy called out, "ask Hannah to keep Billy with her for the moment and come take a look. I found something else."

I reached out for Billy's hand, but Trace beat me to it, lifting him up in his arms. Billy must have been frightened – we all were – because he made no comment and put his arms around Trace's neck.

"Let's go inside the cabin and see if we can find a snack for ourselves and something for the dogs," I told Billy.

Ivy

TROY FOUND MORE paint on the back wall of the chapel that faced a small grove of deciduous trees. We stared at a stick-figure cowboy just below where the stained glass window had been with a bloody bullet hole painted on its forehead. Intimidation, for sure.

"Troy, the game camera! Remember? We forgot to take it home with us when we went back to Montana. We might have another photo of the vandals coming or going," I said.

Excited at the possibility of discovering who was causing all the trouble, we left the dead, stick-figure cowboy and ran as fast as we could to the cabin. There it was, right where we left it. We detached the camera from its spot near the front porch, knowing that finding anything helpful was a long shot.

"The battery likely died before the vandals even returned," Troy said to me. "We'll soon know." He popped open the camera and removed the SD card. "Damn! There's paint covering the lens."

I took the chip from his hand. "I'll grab my laptop from the truck and meet you inside."

After a closer inspection of the camera, Troy noticed that the battery seemed to have some juice left. "Here's hoping the camera snapped some photos before the lens was coated with paint."

With the SD card in place, I crossed my fingers and began to scroll. "Hey, look at this, Troy." There were three photos of two people wearing masks and hoodies. Though better than what we'd seen before, it was not much help.

"Trace, Hannah," I called, "we've got photos of the culprits."

They hurried in from the kitchen with Billy and the dogs. We all stared at the computer screen.

"They're not good, but now we know two people were working together who didn't want to be identified," I said.

"Then why didn't they just smash or steal the camera instead of spray painting it?" Hannah asked.

"Because they're not the sharpest tacks in the tool-box," Trace replied.

So many thoughts raced around in my head. "Maybe they wanted us to know that two people were responsible for the destruction," I said. Still, how did they know we were going to be here? Maybe they didn't know; perhaps it didn't matter as long as the damage was done.

Troy began to pace. "My only deduction is that our vandals are spending most of their time putting their evil ways into practice right here in Wyoming on the gals' property."

I agreed with my man's comment, but who and why? We still had no helpful answers.

CHAPTER FOURTEEN

HANNAH

*H*ours passed slowly, and other than cleaning one of the bathrooms, we accomplished nothing the rest of the gloomy day. Our negativity affected Billy and the dogs too. They were quiet and rarely moved more than their eyeballs as if watching and waiting for us to destroy the lingering despair.

Late that afternoon, Trace's phone rang, Troy's phone rang, the dogs barked, and Billy asked for popcorn. Had the gloom lifted? Or was more bad news about to arrive via cell phones?

Trace went out on the porch to answer his phone; Troy went into the kitchen. I could picture each of them pacing around their space as they talked on their phones.

"I'm going to join Trace on the porch," I said to Ivy.

She popped a Milk Dud into her mouth. "Think I'll take Billy to the kitchen to make popcorn."

We nodded, understanding each other's need to know what the phone calls were about.

After walking out onto the porch, I pretended to play with the dogs, but I listened attentively to Trace's conversation.

"Jane, what a surprise. I'm flattered. You rarely call me." He teased his long-time friend, who was also the sheriff of Stillwater – the town closest to our Colorado ranches – and mother of Callie. Trace quickly pulled the phone away from his face and tapped the speaker icon. I smiled because I knew he *wanted* me to hear Jane's words. He also put a finger to his lips.

"Don't be flattered, though you might be surprised by what I have to say."

"What's wrong?"

"You can stop wondering if Hannah's friend Rick caused any of your problems last fall," she began. "Finally, I received the crime lab report from the Denver office. The DNA from the crash site was definitely Rick's. So now we know for sure neither Rick nor his twin, Rudy, will ever bother you again."

He thanked her for the information and was about to

end when she asked, "Any more problems since that letter showed up?"

Trace stepped away from the dogs and me. Still, I heard him whisper, "What letter?"

I gasped. So happy to see him the day he returned from his trip, I'd forgotten to tell him about the letter. I remembered putting it in a safe place, out of sight. And then forgot all about it. Out of sight, out of mind, I guess. No excuse for that, though.

"You don't know?" Jane asked. "Hannah called three, maybe four weeks back in a tizzy over a letter that had frightened her. I calmed her down, and since you were due back in town the next day, I thought you could handle it. You McAllisters rarely want any help from law enforcement. Besides, U.S. mail is more of a federal issue."

"Okay, Jane. I'll let her know about the DNA results. Thanks for the call."

Trace tapped his phone screen, slid his phone into his pocket, and then turned and glared into my terrified eyes. How could I have been so forgetful and made such a careless error?

Before Trace could ask about the letter, Troy, Ivy, and Billy came outside to join us.

"That was Dad just checking in," Troy said. "He said

he'd heard from a Casper, Wyoming, detective and that Luke and Darrell were still in custody. Apparently, no one was willing to post their bail, so they won't be a problem for quite a while."

I breathed a sigh of relief. I wouldn't have to admit to my omission of information right now.

"Hannah has something to tell us," Trace announced.

I guess I spoke too soon.

"Yes. Yes, I do." I heard myself sigh as a wave of guilt swept over me. "A letter arrived at The Lucky Seven the day Trace left on a three-day trip. He went to investigate Spanish Barbs and BLM wild mustangs. There wasn't much to the letter. Very few words—more like a note."

"Go on," Trace encouraged, his tone softening. "We all need to hear this."

"It was addressed to The McAllisters, and all it said was *Mr. McAllister, Your money or your life.*" Total silence followed. I'd delivered a bombshell and felt absolutely awful that I hadn't told anyone until now. I couldn't imagine what they must be thinking. "Somebody say something."

"Did you notice the postmark?" Ivy asked.

"No, I didn't."

"Do you still have the letter?" Trace and Troy asked simultaneously.

I nodded. "I put it in the drawer of the nightstand by our bed . . . so I wouldn't lose it."

Trace immediately initiated a phone call. We all watched and waited. He seemed to have a plan.

"Rosa, it's Trace. We have a situation here, and I need your help. Ask Harry to drive you to The Lucky Seven. I want you to take the key, go inside, and look for a letter in one of the nightstands by the bed. Ask Harry to bring a gun. No, don't panic. It's just a precaution."

Their conversation lasted a few more minutes. Rosa would call back, hopefully with information about where the letter had originated. We all sat on the porch waiting, knowing the driving time from one ranch to the other. We wouldn't hear from Rosa for at least forty-five minutes.

"Mommy, where is the popcorn?" Billy asked.

"Oh, now I'm the forgetful one," Ivy said. "I'll be right back. Billy, would you come with me? I'll need help carrying our snacks."

"Sure."

Ivy and Troy were so lucky to have Billy in their lives. He was such a delightful child who always wanted to help.

"Bring two bowls and some iced tea," Troy suggested.

"Could I have juice?" Billy asked. "I don't really like tea."

Ivy smiled and said, "This tea will have ice."

He shrugged. "It will still taste like tea." Did I see a little pout on his angelic face?

Trace and I sat quietly, waiting for the snacks to arrive. Though I didn't speak, plenty of thoughts were messing with my mind. I wondered if Trace was angry with me.

Ivy and Billy returned with the goods. Sipping, munching, and crunching would help pass the time. We all dove in and pretended to wait patiently for Rosa's call. Unable to sit still, I let everyone know I would stretch my legs by walking up the long driveway. To distract my thinking, I'd keep my eyes open for plants. After all, I'd only been here during cold months when the only greenery was a few juniper and pine trees.

Trace caught up with me before I'd gone very far. "You know, darlin', with a threatening letter in Colorado, a demolished chapel here in Wyoming, and a recent kidnapping attempt in Montana, we're not out of the dark woods yet. So, ma'am, please humor me just this once and come back to the porch. We should all stick close together until our new villain or villains are no longer a threat."

I stood on tiptoe and kissed my wonderful man on the lips. He was so caring and sensible. Any other man might have been enraged, but not Trace. He took my hand, and we rejoined the popcorn eaters.

"Why do we want to know where the letter was mailed?" I asked as I grabbed a handful of the buttery treat.

Troy stepped off the porch, began to pace, and then answered my question. "Having that information could be helpful. What if it was mailed from the town nearest your ranch, Trace? Or a town near mine?"

"Or there might not be a visible postmark at all. Some of my mail back in Denver arrived that way," Ivy added.

Trace jumped in. "Speculation isn't going to help. We will know more than we know now after Rosa's call."

Trace's phone rang about the same time the popcorn bowls were empty. He nodded, and we knew it was Rosa.

"Well, what's the word? Is there a postmark on the envelope?" He listened. "I see." He listened some more, and I wondered why he hadn't put the phone on speaker so we could all hear what Rosa had to say. That worried me. "Anything seem out of place or odd?" The frustrating silent gaps continued. "Just one more, no, two more things. Please make sure the place is locked up tighter than a barn filled with sweet feed. Then, on your way out, check the mailbox down at the end of the driveway. Leave the junk mail there, but take the rest with you. Call me later if there's anything else I need to know." He tapped the phone screen and put his phone back in his pocket.

"Hey, man. Don't keep us in suspense. Start talking," Troy said impatiently.

"Okay. Here it is. The letter was mailed from Worland."

"Holy crap!" Troy kicked the dirt, obviously not pleased. Even the dogs cowered and put some distance between themselves and the angry cowboy.

With her face frowning, Ivy ded ared to speak up. "What's so bad about Worland?"

Trace knew the answer. "Ladies, Worland is in Wyoming, and it's only about 80 miles north of here."

"And that's not all. The distance between The Lonely Horse Ranch and Worland isn't much further than that. It's just — as the crow flies — south. I'm calling Kitchi." Troy spoke rapidly, his tone tinged with anger.

I was certain we were in for another one-sided phone conversation, but Troy went inside to make his call. Ivy and I waited on the porch for the information his call might provide. Trace grabbed a tennis ball from the truck and played with Billy and the dogs.

Troy's call was a quick one; he returned in a matter of minutes.

"Do you want the bottom line or the long version?" he asked.

"Bottom line," Trace said.

Ivy went in the opposite direction. "Details. I want all the details."

It didn't matter to me. I knew the news was not good no matter how we got it.

"Trace, we received a similar letter with the same postmark. Kitchi found it in Saige's office in the guest registration building. She hadn't opened it thinking it was a personal letter – in a way, it was."

"Similar, but not the same?" I asked.

"What exactly did our note say?" Ivy almost whispered.

Troy kicked at the dirt again, stalling. "It's not really suitable for young ears."

"Then go inside and write it down!" Ivy's voice had returned.

"I can read my name," Billy said.

"I know, sweetie. Your name won't be on this note. But in a few days, I'll teach you to read more words. Okay?" Ivy said sweetly.

The boy seemed satisfied for the moment. Troy gave in to Ivy's demand and went back inside, though not for long. He returned and held the sheet of paper up to Ivy's face. Trace and I stood behind her so we could read the threatening words at the same time.

Mr. McAllister,

Your money or your life.

Had enough yet? I'm on my way.

"It seems to me that our new property is right in the middle of the trouble. Having our own ranch here in Wyoming was just not meant to be. The universe has made that perfectly clear," I said. My words poured out with little thought and a whole lot of fear. Would Ivy disagree or think I was weak?

"I agree with Hannah," Ivy said. "Most of the vandalism has occurred right here. We should put this property up for sale before one or all of us gets hurt."

She took my hand and pulled me inside. I knew we had some decisions to make.

"We could sell the property, but I think we should wait on that decision," I said. Are they doing this

Ivy agreed again. "We have a more important decision to make right now. All of our lives, literally, are at stake."

"Yes. And we need to be as far away from this place as possible."

Surprisingly, Ivy stepped closer and hugged me for the first time. I had no problem hugging her back. She was beginning to feel like the sister I never had.

No way could our double wedding take place here. We had only one intelligent option. It was sad and disappointing, but we both agreed to it. Still holding hands, we stepped back out onto the porch to make our announcement.

We spoke as one voice with the words, "Our July wedding is canceled!"

CHAPTER FIFTEEN

IVY

"*N*ow, we can focus our attention on solving our mysteries, beginning with a list of vandalism, extortion, kidnapping, and possibly murder," Hannah said.

I didn't like the sound of those unlawful acts, but Hannah had a good point. Why wait? We should begin creating this list and facing the facts. Sweeping them under the rug would increase the villains' chance of success.

"The letter writer has to be one of the people that torched the old barn, then destroyed the new chapel. Don't you think so?" I said.

Hannah nodded and added, "That is the only conclusion that makes any sense. Still, the million-dollar question is: Who are they and what do they expect to get?"

We'd all made lists of evil troublemakers who had entered and damaged our lives this past year. I thought we'd decided that they were either dead or in jail. Who did we miss?

When nothing came to mind, I said, "Since we're here, we might as well have a nice dinner together and get some sleep. It's been a long day. In the morning, we could take another stab at making a new list of bad guys and form a plan for the McAllisters' survival. What do you guys think?"

Although the men added a few caveats of their own, which involved assigning tasks, everyone agreed to my idea. Some to be completed before we turned in, others would take place tomorrow after we'd finalized our new list of troublemakers – if that were possible.

For now, we'd focus on making dinner and enjoying each other's company. We'd also keep the doors locked, however, and crack a few windows so we could hear anything odd that might occur outside.

I took care of the baked potatoes and placed them in the oven first thing. As usual, Troy cooked the main course. He broiled the steaks, brushing on his homemade secret sauce and poached the fish with sprigs of rosemary.

The aroma was to die for. I prepared the mac 'n' cheese too.

Trace and Hannah took charge of setting the table and combining lettuce, tomatoes, and pine nuts together for a salad.

"This is an unusual menu. Ugly steaks and swordfish?" Trace commented.

"Troy and I thought we should dine on our best entrées tonight rather than drive them home tomorrow," I said.

"I appreciate your menu and that you remembered I'm somewhat of a vegetarian," Hannah said. "And that I do make exceptions for fish on occasion. I haven't had swordfish in years."

"What's a veg-a-tarin?" Billy asked.

"Hannah doesn't eat meat." I wanted my answer to be short – end of discussion. I saw no need to elaborate.

"Why?"

Hannah jumped in. "It's my personal choice, Billy. Trace avoids broccoli. I'm sure there are some foods that you'd rather not eat."

"Yes. Green peas. They're so gross."

Troy tousled the boy's hair and said, "You're in luck tonight. No green peas but plenty of mac 'n' cheese."

"Yay!"

Troy was the best foster parent in the world; I was

sure of that. I'd hoped for a July wedding so we could move beyond foster parent status and file the adoption papers. No telling what the state agency might do if it discovered that Troy and I had not lived together for at least twenty-four months — the requirement for unmarried couples to foster a child.

Except for the salad, all the food was set on the counter. We served ourselves as if at a buffet, so there were fewer serving dishes to wash. I liked that.

We were all seated at the table with our salad bowls full and our dinner plates piled high when suddenly there was a void. It seemed we all felt it. We missed Kitchi. If he were here, he'd give a blessing. To my knowledge, no one at the table had ever said a prayer before eating, but tonight that was exactly what we needed.

"Let's all hold hands before we eat," Billy said.

We all shrugged, looking at each other. Suddenly, the five year old was in charge.

Hannah was the first to speak. "Okay. Sure."

With our hands joined, Billy said, "Thanks for the horses and the pets and the people and the food. A – men."

"Amen," everyone added.

"Let's eat," said Troy. And eat we did.

I was always amazed by how long it takes to create a

delicious meal and then how fast it disappears. Everyone pitched in clearing the table and washing the dishes.

After dinner, we devoured slices of the no-flour chocolate cake in the living room, and the men began to share their plan for surviving the night.

"Troy and I will unhook the horse trailers, parking them side by side with our trucks to create a barrier in front of the house," Trace said. "I'll sleep in my truck, Troy in his." Though I knew very little sleeping would take place. "The horses will spend the night in their trailers. No one stands a chance of sneaking up on us. If they try, they'll meet with a rude awakening."

I felt my jaw drop just a bit; this was getting serious. Our men's protective nature – which I loved – had morphed into something more akin to combat-ready. What wily tactics had they planned for Hannah, Billy, and me?

"Ladies, while you're closing up the kitchen, we'll be lining up the vehicles and getting the horses settled. We'd like you to sleep in the large bedroom tonight," Troy said. "Once we're ready outside, we'll come back in to close and lock all the windows making sure all is secure and kiss you good night. Then, you'll lock the bedroom door."

Billy was barely awake a few minutes ago, but now his eyes stayed wide open. A new excitement swept over him, and he followed Troy and Trace as they headed for the front door.

"Where are you going, Billy?" I asked.

He shot me an indignant look. "With the men."

Troy picked him up and said softly, "I need you to stay in the house so the women will feel safer, okay? Can you do that? While you're lying in bed, you can listen for the dogs. They'll hang out together and have free run of the house. If anything strange occurs, they'll let you know."

"I got this," Billy said, and we all smiled. The boy was already acting like a McAllister man.

The assigned evening tasks were completed before total darkness obscured the view of our surroundings. Trace and Troy made their rounds, including our good night hugs and kisses. We worried about the men but were glad to be inside with Billy and the dogs, although sleep would be difficult.

"You know, Ivy, I'm usually a positive person, but when Trace held me and kissed me, for a fleeting moment, it felt as if we were kissing for the last time."

"Don't go down that dead-end road, Hannah. There's no point to that." I pretended to be strong, brave, and positive, but I was faking it. Nothing felt good to me either. Even my head ached, and my stomach felt queasy. Morning couldn't get here fast enough. For my own sanity and well-being, I needed to be back at The Lonely Horse Ranch ASAP.

Hannah

IF THE DOGS barked last night, I never heard them. It was the sound of pots and pans clanking in the kitchen that woke me. Dressing quickly, I unlocked and opened the bedroom door leaving Ivy and Billy in bed. The smell of bacon cooking lured me to the kitchen.

There I saw Troy at the stove. He turned around when he heard me and then quickly handed me a slice of crispy-looking bacon. "Tell me what you think of this."

I took a healthy bite and then closed my eyes as it practically melted in my mouth. "I think it's darn good, and I'd like another slice, please."

He informed me that the addition of pure maple syrup drizzles made all the difference in the world. All I knew was that it was the best bacon I'd ever tasted. I started to set the table, but Troy stopped me.

"Paper plates and plastic utensils this morning, Hannah. We are going to have a mini-breakfast of scrambled eggs and bacon and then be on the road," he glanced down at his watch, "in less than forty-five minutes.

Would you please round up the rest of our crew? Trace already fed the dogs, so they're good to go."

"Sure. Happy to do that." And I was, but only because the sooner we had breakfast, the sooner we could leave. I never expected those words to monopolize my thoughts, although there they were flashing like a neon sign within my head.

TRACE REACHED across the center console in our truck to hold my hand. He seemed to feel as bad as I did about calling off the July wedding. I smiled at him, the man of my dreams. In that moment, I loved him more than my dogs, my cows, my horse Lewissa, and even my mom. *Even my mom?* Yes.

Ah, my mother. She'd always warned about men and their downfalls. What would she think of my relationship with Trace? I'd never been in love before, so this would be as new for her as it was for me. If only I had her blessing to marry this wonderful man. I wish she would contact me and let me know where she was. She'd never let this many months go by without at least calling. She knows my cell number.

"A penny for your thoughts," Trace voiced his familiar phrase as he squeezed my hand.

I squeezed back. "Hmm. They're worth more than that. Want to know why?"

"Yes, ma'am."

"I was thinking about how much I love you and want to be your wife . . . and our canceled wedding."

Now, by the look on his face, I could tell that he was the one thinking.

"Not canceled, darlin', just postponed. We could have a fall wedding. You once said fall was your favorite season."

"Yes," I sighed, "that's true."

After reaching into the backseat to give Oatie and Little Charlie a pat on the head and a treat, I closed my tired eyes hoping to banish all the depressing, pessimistic thoughts cluttering my mind.

I twitched, startled by the sound of Trace's phone ringing. The tone of uncertainty in his voice made me wake up quickly. I listened and knew right away something was wrong.

"A detour? To where?" Trace asked. "I see. What's the problem? Will she be all right?" Trace listened. "I'll tell Hannah. Let me know what happens."

Trace pressed a button on the steering wheel to end the call. He turned to me.

"How are you feeling, Hannah?"

"I'm okay, a little tired maybe. Why?"

"Troy is at the emergency room at the small hospital in Buffalo. Ivy's not feeling well."

"That's really odd. I can't imagine her going to a hospital just because she's 'not feeling well.' She's usually so strong and stubborn. And with her EMT background, she often diagnoses and treats herself."

"Maybe it wasn't her idea. I could tell that Troy's concern was intense, over the top for him. He said something about possible food poisoning and wanted me to make sure you were feeling okay."

Trace asked me if Ivy or I had eaten anything unusual last night or this morning. We'd all eaten the same breakfast food. I rethought the events of the evening after we'd locked ourselves in the bedroom. Nope, nothing . . . then an idea.

"I doubt this is important, but after Billy went to sleep, Ivy did hold up a baggie filled with nuts and chocolate. Said she'd found it in the glove box of Troy's truck that afternoon. She'd laughed, saying that she felt like a thief and hoped he hadn't had a special plan for the snack."

"Did you partake in the stolen goods?" Trace said with a grin, his eyes twinkling.

"No. I was too tired and not the slightest bit hungry. But Ivy, in the midst of a major chocolate craving, consumed a few handfuls before making a sour face.

She'd said it tasted old, stale; there was nothing good about it. Still, she planned to put it back in the morning while Troy was cooking so he'd be unaware of her minor indiscretion."

Ivy

I WAS SO AGGRAVATED that I didn't feel like talking, so I let Troy ask the questions while I listened. They say doctors and nurses are the worst patients. You could say that about EMTs too. Lying on a hospital bed was not my idea; I did not need to be here. There was nothing wrong with me.

"I just want to go home, Troy. I'll be fine. Maybe it was something I ate. This too shall pass." I rocked back and forth, holding my midsection tightly, hoping a bite of disagreeable food was the culprit messing with my stomach.

"What do you think, Doc?" Troy asked.

"She has no fever. I doubt it's the flu."

The room went sideways. Which way was up? I tried to force myself to breathe slowly, deeply, but I failed miserably. Then the vomiting began. Faster than a lightning bolt, someone turned me onto my side and thrust a pan near my face. Maybe I'm not okay.

Troy held my hair back and said, "Hang in there, babe. We'll get this bug under control and be home by dinnertime."

Dinnertime. The wrong word to say right now. Another round of vomiting began. I heard the doctor order some blood work and an IV. Hopefully, just saline. I was in no condition to argue with the doctor if it were something else.

Sitting quietly in the corner of the curtain-partitioned cubicle, Billy finally had something to say. "Can you make her better?" he asked the doctor.

"We'll do everything we can, young man," he said and then hurried out of the room to tend to another patient that was just brought in.

Turning toward Troy, Billy had another question. "What's the matter with Mom? She never gets sick."

Troy's phone rang before he could come up with an answer. Just as well. An answer had not yet been found.

"How do you know she never gets sick?"

"She told me," Billy said.

"Oh, okay."

Looking at the screen, Troy said, "It's Trace," and switched the phone to speaker mode. "Hey brother, I don't have any news about—"

"How long has that bag of nuts and chocolate been in your glove box?" Trace asked.

I hoped the glimmer of guilt I felt didn't show on my face. Why was Trace bringing up a bag of stale munchies?

"I know nothing about a bag of snacks in my truck."

"It's there," I said, knowing my tone was riddled with guilt. "I ate some of it last night and had a few more bites when I woke up today. I put it back in the truck this morning while you were cooking."

With a smile on his little face, Billy added, "I saw a bag like that, but not in the truck."

"Where did you see—" The group's nut-bag conversation paused when the nurse came in, though I heard Troy mumbling into his phone. "Got to go. I'll call you back, Trace."

Billy watched the nurse's every move.

She gave me an injection to minimize my nausea and then hooked me up to an IV. I began to feel a bit better almost immediately.

"So, Billy," I said, "Where did you see that baggie?" I prayed that he wouldn't say he saw it in the bedroom last night.

"In Oatie's mouth. He found it when he went out back to his poop spot." Billy appeared to be delighted at having an answer to the question.

"Did you put it in the truck?" Troy asked.

The boy's delightful expression morphed into one of worry, and he shook his head.

I tried to smile and asked sweetly, "Then, where is it now?"

He stared at the floor and slowly pulled an almost empty bag of nuts and chocolate from his pocket.

My missing strength suddenly surged back. The mamma bear in me shoved my illness aside. "Did you eat some of the treats? I know you like chocolate too."

"I was going to, but I spilled most of it on the ground, in the dirt. Then it was time for dinner, so I shoved the baggie into my pocket. I'm sorry. I should have given all the treats to you."

"Troy, hand me your phone and go check the truck for that bag. Bring it in if it's there," I ordered.

Troy bolted out of the room, and I called Hannah. "Hi. It seems there may have been two bags of snacks. We're checking that out now. One of us will call you again later when we know something."

"We're halfway home, but we're so worried about you. We could turn around and drive north to Buffalo," Hannah said.

"No. Absolutely not. We'll be out of here soon. The injection and the IV are working well. I'll be okay. But thanks. Go home. We'll call if there is anything significant to tell you."

Troy returned with the bag, so now there were two for sure. He let me know that Shadow and Tracker were doing fine. Billy sat back on his chair, I sat up in bed, and Troy paced as best he could in this tiny, curtained cubical.

"Maybe these were simply snacks the workers left behind," I said.

"Do you really believe that?"

"I want that to be the truth, but no, I don't suppose I do."

Of course, it could not have happened that way. Someone had to place it in the truck. And, if my brain was functioning properly, I figured it must have been put there in the past 24 hours. But who? And why? Two questions we kept asking over and over.

The doctor returned. "You're looking better already, Ms. Radcliff. If your blood work comes back and it's within normal ranges, I'll be able to release you by the end of the day."

"We may have found the cause of Ivy's distress," Troy said as he held up the two bags of nuts and chocolate. "She did consume some of these treats, and they might be rancid."

The doctor nodded, grabbed both bags, and sniffed their contents. "I'll take these to our lab."

Now, Troy held one of my hands, Billy held the other, and we waited.

CHAPTER SIXTEEN

HANNAH

W e drove in silence except for the country music playing softly on the radio. I don't recall falling asleep, but suddenly, I woke up and realized that the truck was coming to a stop. I knew we were halfway home when I saw the two-lane, winding road cutting through a pine forest.

"What's the matter? Why are we stopping?" I asked Trace with panic in my voice. Clearly, I was still on edge from the events of the past 24 hours.

"Everything is okay. The animals and I need to stretch our legs, and this looked like a good spot for a short walk. It provides some shade for the horses and some privacy for us. It's perfect. Come on. I have some questions to ask you."

"All right. I can't shake this sleepy feeling, though."

"A short walk in the fresh air is exactly what you need."

"I hope you're right." I wasn't merely sleepy; it was more than that. But what?

It took Trace a few minutes to unload the horse. The dogs unloaded themselves and kept busy sniffing every tree, bush, and wildflower. In the past, others must have chosen this spot for a rest too. Someone had taken the time to make a bench from a fallen tree trunk. I took advantage of that.

Trace walked his horse around before securing it to a nearby tree. Then he returned to the truck.

"Trace? What are you doing?"

"Just getting my phone, some water for the animals, and a cold soda for us."

He joined me on the bench, and I said, "Questions? You have questions for me?"

"I'm just curious about the plans you and Ivy made for the wedding. You hadn't shared much information with us guys. We'd have been married fairly soon if the chapel hadn't been destroyed."

He was right about that. "What do you want to know?

Nothing we planned will happen now anyway. Someday we'll make new plans, but everything will be different."

"I get that. Still, let's brainstorm a bit while we're sitting here. You know, for the future. What would your perfect wedding look like? You know, a take two, a second chance."

"It would be small, casual, kind of country with wildflowers."

"That's it?"

"Yes, Trace. That's pretty much it. But it's too soon for this discussion—" I stopped almost involuntarily. My breathing became very deep and rapid. "I'm not feeling so good," I said between breaths as I looked at Trace. It was quickly apparent that I was hyperventilating. There was no stopping it.

"Don't move. I'll be right back," he said and swiftly loaded up the horse and the dogs and then came back for me. He took my hand as I stood, but I must have needed more support than that. Dizziness, like never before, invaded my body, I collapsed in his arms, and my world turned dark.

The next thing I knew, I was looking up at a clear blue sky, and my legs felt scratchy from the grass I was lying on. I turned my head slightly and saw Trace leaning over me with a smile.

"Welcome back, darlin'," he said. "It's been a long time since you've had one of your fainting spells. At least you recovered from this one quickly. Did I cause that with my questioning about the wedding?"

"I doubt that. I'm still a little dizzy, and I just want to go home."

Trace picked me up and carried me to the truck. I appreciated having such a kind, strong man in my life. I'm a lucky wo—"Oh, no. I think I'm going to be sick," I blurted out. I could barely say the words as I felt my stomach beginning to erupt.

Trace set my feet on the ground and continued to hold me securely upright. In seconds, my breakfast began its journey through the air. That's when Trace's cell phone rang.

"Get it," I squeaked out breathlessly.

"Nope. You're my priority. They can leave a message. That's what voicemail is for."

"But what if—"

"No buts allowed. Let me know when you feel ready to get back in the truck."

Though feeling weak, I was able to stand leaning up against the truck.

Trace handed me a water bottle from the cooler that was in the truck's back seat, and I took a few sips. If that stayed down, I'd agree to get on the road again. After fifteen minutes of inhaling fresh air and knowing my stomach had to be empty by now, I got back into the truck. Trace pressed the speaker button on his phone, and we listened to the voicemail Troy had left.

"Turns out there was a second bag of nuts and chocolate. The doctor sent them to the hospital's lab to see what they might find. If Hannah had even one bite of that stuff, you'd better get her to a hospital too. After smelling the contents of the bag, the doc whispered to me that—"

The message cut off, stopped dead. "Is your phone the problem or his? He would not stop in the middle of a message like that."

"Maybe it's just a cell range issue or his battery. You didn't eat any of those nuts, right?"

"No. Ivy had several handfuls, but I ate nothing from the bag."

"Good. Let's head out. I'll try calling Troy just as soon as I see a strong signal on my phone, and you are going to have a complete physical with the McAllister family doctor as soon as we can schedule it."

Ivy

How would I feel without the IV or the nausea injection? With them, I felt good enough to leave. But was that good feeling false, a mere temporary cover-up of my actual condition? I wanted to know. I'll ask the doctor the next time I see him. Whoa! Speak of the devil.

"I have some good news and bad news," the doctor said as he pulled the curtain to my cubicle closed. "As you suspected, the nuts were rancid. You see, when the oils in nuts oxidize, they create a range of spoilage molecules with funky names – *pentanal, 2-ethyl furan, hexanal, trans-2-octenal* – and even funkier smells. Your discomfort from those nuts will pass, and I can give you something to help that along."

I wondered if that were both the good and bad news.

"We suspect traces of cyanide in the bags too, but further testing is needed to know for sure. I'd like to do more blood work before you leave. Any chance you could be pregnant?"

"Nope, none."

"Good."

I relaxed against the bed's pillow, but only for a second. I remembered that Billy said he didn't eat anything from the bags, but I wondered if he had touched those nuts. Oh, dear.

"Doctor, would it be harmful to merely touch but not ingest the rancid nuts?"

"Poison is not my expertise. Why don't you give the poison control center a call?"

"Where are those bags, doctor?" Troy asked with a tone of authority. "I'd like to have them back."

"I'm afraid I can't help you with that. The police have them now, and eventually, they will want to talk to you."

"Dammit! Here we go again," he whispered to me.

"What will they do with them?" Though weak, I managed a firm, convincing tone.

"They'll be destroyed once they've reached a conclusion or a dead end. You do realize that if there really are traces of cyanide in those bags, someone was attempting to make you quite ill or worse. And that's a crime."

The doctor left, and then a med-tech walked in and drew some blood.

Hannah

I ASKED Trace if he wanted to call Troy back or if I should call Ivy's phone. When he grinned and said we should flip a coin, I shook my head and called Ivy. Relief washed over me when she answered.

"Hey dear friend, I hear you're in the hospital. Are you doing all right?"

"Hi, Hannah. Yes, I'm better. My nausea and

vomiting were from those darn nuts. And get this: the doctor said there might be traces of cyanide in the bags, which are now in police custody."

"Oh, my God! Police custody?"

That got Trace's attention. "Who is in police custody?" he asked.

"It's not a who. It's a what."

I put my hand over the speaker and turned to Trace. "It was the nuts," I told him, "and cyanide might be involved."

After I was sure Ivy was okay, I returned to a bit of girl talk.

"Has Troy been asking you about our wedding plans?"

"No, not really. He did say that we should run away and elope – I think he was joking – but maybe he had an ulterior motive and wanted me to talk about new plans. When I shrugged and said okay to eloping, he changed the subject."

When Ivy asked how I was doing, I relayed my dismal story of what just happened on the side of the road and assured her that *nuts* were not part of it. Perhaps, the presence of crazy, nutty people might have set off this attack of anxiety. But was anxiety the correct self-diagnosis? Stomach upset had never occurred before.

"Hey, Hannah. Troy just asked if I wanted to get out

of here. I gave him an affirmative nod, and I'm pulling out my IV as we speak. We're making a break for it. I'll call you when we get home."

I overheard Troy say, "Ivy's IV is out!" I could hear all of them, including Billy, laughing.

THE FAIRY TALE, THE MEN IN BLACK, AND THE EMPTY CHAIR

CHAPTER SEVENTEEN

IVY

*B*arely a week after my hospital experience, Troy and I had finally relaxed enough to take a soak in our spa. We tucked Billy safely into bed and headed toward heated bliss. It was conveniently located and almost attached to the master bedroom. In fact, all I had to do was look through the open archway, and I could see the huge spa while lying in bed.

Tonight, I needed nothing more than the hot water, the bubbling jets, the music, and my man. Those few days of feeling physically horrible enlightened me with a new and solid appreciation of healthy days and my wonderful life. Never again would I take them for granted.

I sat on the bench that just barely kept my head above

water until Troy pulled me under so that we were sitting on the floor of the hot tub. We revisited the art of kissing without the benefit of air. We came up sputtering, laughing, and kissing the easy way. I had so many things to appreciate.

"Ivy, babe, I know we'll reschedule our wedding eventually, but I'm curious. What did you and Hannah have planned? No, I've got a better question. What would our perfect wedding in the future look like?"

Since the destruction of our beautiful little chapel and the unresolved nut mystery, planning a wedding was the furthest thing from my mind. And for now, I wanted to keep any such thoughts away, far away. And that is precisely what I told Troy.

"I get that, no planning right now. Can you tell me what you and Hannah had hoped for?"

"Okay. That I can do. We didn't agree on much, though we came to a compromise giving each of us some of what we wanted. I desired something a little more formal, with a few more people and long white wedding dresses. And I'd wanted to carry a bouquet with a mix of lavender and white roses. In other words, an almost traditional wedding in spite of its remote location and the small chapel."

Of course, that was before everything changed. No

way did I wish to exchange vows where so much destruction had taken place.

"When do you think you'll be ready to discuss our wedding plans?"

"Troy, with all that's happened lately, how can you even ask that?" I felt exasperated.

No winking, no sign of a loving smile. Disappointment, or was it anger, radiated from him.

"So, you've given up thinking about marrying me?" he asked defensively.

That did it. My less than perfect side boiled up, and I turned my back on him. Why would he ask that? Was he hoping I'd say yes? Or was he giving up on me? I have been a bit of a bitch lately. Before I said anything I would regret, I decided to get out of the water. With water sloshing off of me, I grabbed a towel and began to walk away. By the time I reached the archway dividing the spa from our bedroom, my better self had returned. *I've got to get a handle on these mood swings.*

I stepped slowly to the king-size bed and sat still wrapped in a towel. Looking up, I saw that Troy had gotten out of the spa too. He'd wrapped a towel around his waist and was walking toward me.

I took in a deep breath. "Oh, Troy. I'm sorry. I don't know what came over me."

There we stood, about ten feet apart, just looking at

each other. Then, without actually thinking, I ran to him –
lost my towel along the way– jumped up, wrapped my
arms around his neck and my legs around his waist, and
planted a kiss on his mouth.

"This is nice, but I don't want us to crash down on the
hard tile floor. So, next time, could you forewarn me and
say something like, oh, I don't know . . . incoming?"

"Well, then. There are times when you should say the
same to me."

Troy frowned, but after a few thoughtful seconds
passed, he winked. "Yes, ma'am."

I found myself vividly conscious of his virile appeal
as he gently eased me down onto the bed. It wasn't long
before he whispered, "Incoming."

CHAPTER EIGHTEEN

IVY

A few days before the end of July, Troy watched as I dressed for the extravagant evening he and Trace had planned. He told me to wear the most formal dress I owned. The only formal dress I owned was the white silk dress I'd purchased to wear for the original chapel wedding. With no new date set, I was happy to have an occasion to wear it. At least it won't go to waste.

One thing Hannah and I agreed on was that we were not quite ready to plan another wedding. The future of our ranch was still up in the air, and the cloud of unsolved mysteries hung heavy over our heads.

I was of a mind to quietly sneak off and elope – not

much planning involved for that. The sooner we married, the sooner we could adopt Billy.

"I want to get this show on the road," Troy said out of the blue. "How about an October wedding?"

I couldn't bring myself to say anything. I was done, so the discussion about weddings shut down completely.

"I still think this evening's dinner with Trace and Hannah is way over the top," I said as I slipped on my silver pumps and gave myself one last look in the mirror.

"What's over the top about dressing up, then flying in a private jet to another state for a fancy dinner?"

"Uh, everything."

"Come on, babe. It's going to be a blast! It's a quick flight; you won't have time to look down. Besides, you and Hannah deserve something special after all you've been through. This is what Trace and I came up with. Don't rain on our well-planned parade."

"All right," I said, turning toward him. "You do look amazing too. Where have you been hiding your black tux and your ultra-shiny black cowboy boots?"

Troy winked and said, "I don't have to answer that." We were in one of our bantering moods.

"Fine. Then answer this. How do I look?" My dress felt a little tighter than the day I'd purchased it. My fault, for sure. I hadn't been as regular with my workouts lately.

As soon as we get back from this extravagant dinner, I'll be hitting the gym every day.

He stood back and studied me. "You, my dear, are a combination of visions: a beautiful Hollywood star and the sweetest angel there ever was."

He'd rendered me speechless, took my hand, and escorted me outside to . . . a limo?

"I thought Kitchi was going to drive us to the small airfield where our lightweight, speedy, flying carriage awaited."

Troy had an answer for that "He was, but as it turned out, he had other plans."

That was weird. Kitchi would do anything for Troy and vice versa. We didn't talk much on the thirty-minute drive to the airfield where several ranchers housed their private planes. Troy, although holding my hand, avoided eye contact with me. His face had a proud expression, but I detected a hint of a smile there too.

"Here we are, babe, about to be leavin' on a jet plane. With clear skies the whole way, you'll be able to see for miles . . . but you don't have to look."

After the plane crash experience, I tried blocking my fear of heights from my mind, a coping mechanism that had worked – though not very well – for me. Flying on a huge passenger plane was bad enough, but a small jet? I began to take slow, steady breaths anticipating feelings of anxiety and hoping to keep them suppressed. My fear was unacceptable; I didn't want to be afraid of anything, ever.

After we'd returned from Clint's Winter Challenge last Christmas, I came up with a plan to lessen my fear of heights, though I kept that plan to myself. It was simple, and I was determined. I'd found a tall ladder behind the barn that housed the gym and Troy's plane before it crashed. Whenever no one was around, I'd set the ladder up against the wall of the barn and climb up and down several times. I almost gave up after my first attempt but didn't. My anxiety, at least for ladder climbing, seemed to lessen. Today I prayed my learning would carry over to flying high above the ground. We'd soon find out.

Hannah, looking so pretty in her long wildflower dress, stood just inside the jet, waving. "Can you believe it?" she called out. "This is no ordinary dinner and a movie date. We're on a formal dinner and a private jet ride double date." She laughed and looked so happy.

I walked up the few steps to the jet's door, then ducked and stepped inside. We hugged and took our seats next to each other as the engines began to roar. Trace suggested we gals take the window seats. I passed on his offer, knowing I would not be looking out any of the jet's windows. I got no arguments regarding my decline of the seat with a view, so I let the seating subject drift away. But I had questions.

"Hannah, do you know anything about where we are going? Troy has given me no clues."

She shrugged and shook her head, showing no sign of frustration at the lack of knowledge.

"This is the first mystery date I've ever been on. I didn't know there was such a thing until now. Don't you think this is exciting?" Hannah said.

I did, and I was certain my enthusiasm would surface just as soon as we touched down.

Hannah

STEPPING CAREFULLY from the jet with Trace's guidance – wearing a long dress and heels called for some help – I gazed at the most spectacular rustic structure and majestic landscape I'd ever seen. Noticing four other jets even smaller than ours parked off to the side of the short runway, I assumed this must be a popular destination for the wealthy. I didn't see any cars, though.

Once we were out of the jet and our feet on the ground, a man wearing a tuxedo pulled up and drove us in a large, golf cart-type vehicle toward the entrance of the building. He seemed overdressed to be a driver for such a wild, rustic-looking establishment in this gorgeous middle-of-nowhere location. He stopped halfway to let several moose walk by.

"Do you think those are real moose or merely fake ones like Disneyland might have to create some wild and wooly charm?" I asked Ivy, who seemed just as unsure as I was.

Either way, we turned our heads to observe them.

"Ladies, I guarantee those are real, live animals," the driver said.

Our men were unfazed by the beasts. Seeing them in the wild, up so close, was thrilling, but wasn't that dangerous too? "Sir, are we safe being so near those animals? I thought moose were aggressive and danger-ous," I said.

"You're right about that, ma'am. They can be. Just don't make sudden moves or loud noises when they're nearby."

The moose ambled off as if we weren't even there, and then the driver continued toward our destination.

"The owners here are animals lovers and allow any and all wild animals to roam freely on their 300-acre property," the driver said. "No fences anywhere."

Ivy and I had a simultaneous jaw-dropping, eyc-widening moment.

The driver chuckled. He'd likely seen similar reac-tions from other guests before. "I need to stress, though, to be careful when they're nearby. I'm sure you read that in the agreement you signed when making your unusual reservation."

I turned toward Trace and said softly but with great emphasis, "Our unusual reservation? What is going on here? Aren't we a bit over dressed for hanging out with wild animals?"

Before Trace answered my question, the driver said, "Here we are. Enjoy your stay."

Two tuxedo-clad men greeted us. One said, "Welcome, McAllister family. We're honored to have you at The Hideaway Inn." The other said, "Follow me."

I looked at Ivy. We were both in a state of shock and wonder. I moved closer to her and whispered, "Feels like we're living in a fairy tale."

"Yes, I agree. But are we in Cinderella or Hansel and Gretel?"

"Perhaps a little bit of both."

I think the term *great room* was invented right here. Oh, my gosh. This room, this lobby, no matter what one calls it, was beyond great. So huge, so rustic, yet pristine and elegant. Most of the walls were hand-carved flat logs, a stone fireplace took up one entire wall, and the windows offered views of pines, cottonwoods, and jagged peaks.

With plenty of distance between the moose and us, we

relaxed. "Now I'm curious about what's for dinner," I said. We both giggled. Those giggles were short-lived and replaced by our jaws dropping again when we saw another couple approaching.

"Finally, you're here. We were so anxious to see the four of you," Alice gushed as she gave each of us a hug. Clint shook his sons' hands. "I thought this day would never get here, but here it is."

I looked up at Trace, hoping for an explanation.

"We invited Mom and Dad to join us for this special evening," Trace said.

"We wouldn't have missed this for the world," Alice replied, smiling from ear to ear.

It was just a fancy dinner, albeit under confusing circumstances. I turned to avoid detection and whispered to Ivy again, "Did you see Clint give his wife the elbow just then?"

"Sure did."

Alice reached toward me and fluffed up my hair and then smoothed Ivy's a bit.

The woman had an edge, a controlling way of moving through life. We knew that. Oh, well – so much for a romantic, fairy tale dinner. Still, it would be unusual and fun.

Trace and Troy must have thought their mom was

acting weird too because rather than linger, they announced, "We should get going."

Dinner for six, here we come. Another unexpected guest approached us as we made our way through the great room and toward the dining area's double doors.

"Kitchi?" Ivy and I said at once.

"You're both looking lovely as always."

I turned to Trace, and Ivy turned to Troy. And again, we both spoke as one.

"What is going on here?"

Clint and Alice excused themselves and went ahead of us into the dining area.

Trace grinned; Troy winked. Ivy and I waited for an answer.

"What's going on?" Trace asked with a smirk. "A wedding."

Now, Ivy's high-heeled shoe tapped an impatient beat. "I was under the impression we were invited to an unforgettable dinner with you and Trace, not attending someone's wedding. Who's getting married?"

"You and me," Troy said.

Ivy's wide-open eyes held a look of shock. Pretty sure mine did too. All of my immediate thoughts made little sense. Was I here to attend Troy and Ivy's wedding? Why didn't someone tell me about this?

Trace took my hand, cleared his throat, and asked, "Want to know who else is getting married?"

He must have seen the frustrated look on my face because he didn't wait for me to come up with an answer.

"You and I, Hannah."

No one spoke. The silence seemed to go on forever. I assumed the men were waiting for our reactions. Well, they got to see our jaws drop, Ivy's foot stop tapping, and my head shake. None of which was a pretty sight, nor the way two brides-to-be should look or act.

"We felt bad when your small, peaceful chapel was vandalized beyond repair. We knew you'd already begun to make plans for a simple double wedding there, and we wanted to do something nice for both you, for all of us," Troy explained. "This is what we came up with."

"But weddings take planning and flowers and legal paperwork," I finally managed to say.

"You got that right, darlin'," Trace said.

Troy added, "Believe me, it wasn't easy. Mom and Dad helped out." His worried expression faded, and a subtle, easy smile played at the corners of his mouth. "You're both in for a really big surprise."

Bigger than an out-of-state, secret, double wedding? That's not possible. I was sure of that.

"Excuse me, gentlemen," Kitchi said. "May I have a moment of your time?"

"First, I'd like to know where we are," I said. "I'm pretty sure we're in Wyoming. I could see the rough, jagged mountain ranges in the distance."

"And the doormen welcomed us to The Hideaway Inn," Ivy added.

"That's right, but still, where are we?" I asked again.

Trace scratched his head. "I'm not exactly sure."

Ivy and I looked at each other. "Unacceptable."

The guys struggled for words but finally explained that we were not in any town; we were sort of out in the wilderness between things. In one direction was Yellowstone National Park, in another was Jackson Hole, and the Grand Tetons were not far away. We could live with that.

The three men walked away. Ivy and I discussed this wild and crazy plan we were a part of, wondering all the while what Kitchi's role in the *really big surprise* was.

"Are we good with this?" Ivy asked.

"If the chapel hadn't been vandalized, we'd already be married," I reminded her. Was I giving in to this plan? It sounded better by the minute. Of course, I was. I couldn't wait to be married to the man of my dreams.

"True," she said. " The men have gone to a lot of trouble to put this together. And I must say that we do look terrific."

I chuckled and said, "Yes, we absolutely do."

"It's so shocking, surprising, that's all," Ivy said. "My

only real objection is that Billy isn't here. I wanted him to be with us when we tied the knot."

Ivy had a good reason to call this off. I wouldn't blame her if she did. "Maybe this isn't as real and legal as the guys think is, and later you can get married again at The Lonely Horse Ranch with Billy as the best man," I suggested.

"You're right, Hannah. So . . . are we good with this?"

We stared at each other with our eyes wide open, then nodded.

"Let's do it!"

CHAPTER NINETEEN

IVY

"Ready or not, here they come." I watched Troy, my husband-to-be, as he walked toward me with Trace at his side. His usual, confident stride appeared hesitant.

"Hannah, what would you think of stalling for a minute or two before giving them our *let's do it* answer?"

"I think that is a splendid idea."

There we stood, looking serious as they approached us. No smiles yet. We were saving them for a little later. An awkward silence prevailed, lessened slightly by the return of Kitchi. I assumed he would function as Troy's best man, and that was why he was here. But then I wondered why Kitchi didn't bring Billy with him. He should be here too. Something was off.

Hannah whispered to me, "I think two minutes are almost up." Then, before I could stop her, she said to the men, "We're ready. Let's get this wild wedding started."

Everything happened so fast. Trace and Troy hurried back down the hallway they'd just come from, and Clint was suddenly at Hannah's side. He reached up and took her arm, saying, "Are you ready to roll?"

And then Kitchi took mine. I asked him softly, "Does my scar show too much?" I knew he was the only one who would tell me the truth.

"Miss Ivy, you are as beautiful as ever. You possess Bear Power now." I could tell by the all-knowing look in his eyes that he meant that.

Waiting outside the double doors, Alice handed each of us a bouquet. Delicate wildflowers for Hannah and a mixture of lavender and white roses for me. Someone knew us well, listened well, and had done their research, though Alice likely made the purchase.

The two men in black opened the double doors to what we'd been led to believe was the dining area. If this was the resort's dining room, it had been majestically transformed. No sign of tables or food service items, but we saw several rows of chairs that appeared to be handcrafted from Aspen branches. Potted aromatic fir trees bordered the seating area.

The four of us remained side by side at the doorway, waiting. From that distance, Hannah and I gazed in awe at our surroundings. Soon we'd walk down the forest green, velvet aisle where Troy and Trace waited for us to join them.

"Look, Hannah. The decorative arch they're standing in front of resembles one wall of our little chapel before it was destroyed," I said.

"I know! There's even a similar stained glass window hanging there too. Our men are amazing! They thought of everything and then some."

"And the people – oh, my gosh – I wasn't expecting guests." I was crying already, and I am not the crying type.

Hannah paused, then asked, "What are we waiting for?"

I wondered the same thing. Kitchi gave us the short answer. "The flower girl and the ring bearer."

Saige, The Lonely Horse Ranch's registrar, dashed up. "I'm so sorry. A couple of moose walked right in front of us as we made our way from the staging cabin. So we had to wait until they wandered off. By then, we needed a pit stop. But here we are."

She placed Ella with a basket of flower petals at the

head of the procession and little Billy, carrying a pillow holding four rings, right behind her. Both children turned to smile and wave at me.

Then Billy said, "I'm not a bear or . . . but I do have the rings."

Both Hannah and I stifled our laughter and gave him a thumbs up.

Music began to play, and we proceeded very slowly down the aisle. Tossing petals takes time. To my delight, the song the trio played was "Can't Help Falling In Love With You." Ah, if only Elvis were here to sing it.

Hannah

I WAS a touch envious of Ivy. Seeing little Billy sent Ivy over the moon with happiness. If only I had some family here, I'd feel a similar joy.

Halfway down the aisle, my eyes remained on Trace, the man of my dreams. He was all I really needed. But why was his finger pointing to my left and his face grinning? One should not point or grin at a wedding. Curious, I glanced to my left. Scanned the guests and . . . there sat my recently discovered grandparents, Linda and Lyle Langford. I blinked back tears of joy. I had family at my wedding after all.

Finally, at the altar, Clint relinquished my arm to Trace and rolled back to sit with Alice. Kitchi gave Ivy away to Troy and took his place in front of the four of us. It seemed he'd be officiating the ceremony—a man of many talents, for sure.

Little Ella stood next to me. Apparently, the flower girl doubled as my bridesmaid. Billy stood by Troy. He also had two jobs – ring bearer and best man. I hoped there was a photographer present. I'd want to revisit this precious scene often.

The music faded, and Kitchi began with the typical wedding vows. When the time was right, he asked us to face our partners. I gazed into my love's eyes, mesmerized, ready to do my part. I felt as if I were weightless and floating on air . . . until I got a glimpse of one of the doormen dressed in black standing in front of a single side door not far from us. He looked almost like a limo driver, although a little too serious for a wedding ceremony.

Trace gently lifted up my chin. His words, "Well, do you?" brought me back to reality quickly. I'd missed my cue. I heard a few giggles from the wedding party, and then Kitchi restated his question.

"Do you, Hannah, take this man . . ."

He and Trace had my full attention. Nothing could distract me now. "Yes, I do, I really do with all my heart."

When Kitchi asked for our rings, Billy took a few steps to stand right in front of him and held up the ring pillow. Ella tapped my arm and pointed at my bouquet. Of course, it was time for her to hold it. In my own defense, there had been no rehearsal dinner, and I'm a first-time bride. After saying all the usual words and with rings on our fingers, it was Troy and Ivy's turn to do the same.

Kitchi added a few Native American wedding vows. "Trace and Hannah, Troy and Ivy, we honor mother-earth and ask for your marriage to be abundant and grow stronger through the seasons. We honor fire, wind, and water. With all the forces of the universe, we pray for harmony and true happiness as we forever grow young together."

We had our first kiss as husband and wife. Troy and Ivy did too. Kitchi asked us to face our friends, our guests, and then he thanked them for coming. He ended his official responsibilities with a few words for everyone. The sweet, haunting sound of a pan flute accompanied him.

"Listen to the wind, it talks. Listen to the silence, it speaks. Listen to your heart, it knows."

He gave the trio a nod. They played the traditional "Wedding March" by Mendelssohn for the recessional but with an unusual twist. A little bit country and a little bit Native American. All in all, a joyful sound. Trace took my hand, and we headed back down the aisle. Troy and Ivy were close behind, and Ella and Billy followed. Smiling at Linda and Lyle when we passed by, I noticed tears in their eyes and blew them a kiss. There would be time to talk later.

Halfway down the aisle, Trace said, "Look who's sitting next to Lester."

When I didn't see Ella's grandfather right away – we'd never actually met before, but I'd seen a photo – Trace's smile widened, and he pointed subtly toward the right. What I saw took my breath away. Was I dreaming? Hallucinating? This cannot be real.

"Mom?" I said softly.

Lillian's reply came in the form of a nod and a genuine smile.

"But how—"

"She'll meet you out in the lobby, Lillian. Later, you can tell your daughter all about your new life."

More breathless than before, I was delighted and felt lucky to still be standing. In the past, such emotional surprises had sent me reeling, even fainting. This perfect day just kept getting better. As we approached the double doors that led us back to the inn's main lobby, the two men in black – I giggled every time those words popped up – reached for the door handles, but, to everyone's surprise, the doors flung open without their help.

Shocked, I screamed. We all screamed. It was too late to do much else. Two masked intruders pointed guns at us. My husband moved swiftly and stood between me and the guns.

"Everybody down on the floor, don't move. We're only here for the McAllister brothers and their new wives." The slightly taller one spoke, his voice deep and demanding.

"And don't even think about being a hero. We hate heroes. The day won't end well for anyone here that tries to stop us." Culprit number two spoke with a gruff, female voice. The intruders wore masks and hoodies, making it impossible to identify either. Hmm.

So many thoughts swirled in my head. Were Ella and Billy all right? Could these be the same people who attempted to kidnap Billy not long ago? I thought we'd eliminated them from our list of vandals. Or had they sent others to help nab the child for them? I wish I knew. Then I remembered the dark, blurry game camera photos.

"I know you can put on a fake cry, but can you fake fainting?" Trace whispered over his shoulder. "This would be a good time to faint due to a heart problem."

I nodded, gave a weak whimper, and slowly sank toward the floor. Trace broke my fake fall and then kneeled at my side, distressed and vocal about my brand new, imaginary heart condition. Now Troy and Ivy had a good view of our intruders, but what would our next move be?

Ivy

THIS IS BAD, really bad. At least one of the wedding guests reacted quickly and pulled Ella and Billy from the aisle and into the small group of guests crouching by their seats. Thank God the kids were out of sight. I hoped they were lying flat on the floor hidden by other adults and the wooden chairs.

Looking straight ahead at the guns pointed right at us, Troy whispered without moving his lips. A new talent he hadn't yet shared with me.

"Do you see Dad? Are he and Mom still in the aisle?"

I didn't possess his ventriloquial talent, so I covered my mouth as if yawning and replied, "I only see Alice."

"Damn! That's what I was afraid of. Dad—always the hero. We've got to take some action before he does."

Trace, still on the floor with Hannah, looked up at the thugs. "What do you want from us?"

"We want what we've always wanted," the man demanded. "To make you suffer, make you miserable, and Hannah's lottery winnings – all of it. But now, we want a major contribution from the McAllisters too. It's the least you can do to save your lives," he taunted.

"Who said anything about a lottery win?" Trace asked. "And, even if there were such a thing, how would you know about it?"

"We're not telling you nothin'," the taller of the two snarled.

"You murdered our son. That's all you need to know."

"Shut the fuck up, Rachel."

Now we knew we were dealing with one man and one woman named Rachel.

That must have been the last straw for Hannah because she sprang up and shouted, "You'll never get away with this."

"Oh, what have we here?" Rachel said. "A pretty little liar? You sure recovered fast from your fainting spell and your delicate heart." The woman tapped her chest, mocking.

Before Trace could stop her, Hannah lunged toward that woman and spat in her face.

"I've got a gun, you idiot. And I'm wearing a mask. See?"

"Sure do. I also see the droplets below your mask." Hannah tapped her own face just to the side of her lips. The woman did the same. Discovering she'd been hit with spit, she went into a rage and then grabbed and held Hannah by the hair.

"You're running out of time. Here's the deal," the man snapped. "All four of you are gonna walk through these doors, then out the main entrance. Then, we're all gonna hurry to the jet that has its engine running."

"Who's your pilot?" Troy asked. I knew he was just stalling.

"Tom, don't tell him. He don't need to know," Rachel said, seething through her teeth.

Oh, geez. Not another plane ride orchestrated by crazy criminals that want us dead. Although, they will need to keep us alive until they have the money they want. With my fear of heights, a typical plane ride was tough enough, but this? Troy put his arms around me, understanding the horrific memories of the plane crash we both shared.

"Get movin' before I start shooting," Tom ordered.

"Let go of my daughter and drop your guns before I start shooting. Do it!"

Although she couldn't see who was speaking, Hannah clearly recognized the voice. "Mom? You brought a gun to my wedding?"

"Damn straight, I did. Comes with my new job."

There we were with two guns in front of us and one behind. If bullets were fired, we stood right in their path.

That's when I noticed Clint, in his wheelchair, parked in the lobby a mere eight to ten feet behind the intruders, with Kitchi at his side. Their presence was still unnoticed by the criminals. I knew they'd do their best to block the intruders' path if they tried to leave with us as their captives. Troy and Trace nodded subtly at each other and then gave exaggerated nods to the large tuxedoed doormen who'd been inching their way toward the thugs hoping to be undetected until it was time to strike.

The two men lunged at the intruders, and Hannah managed to pull free, though during the scuffle, shots were fired. Trace helped Hannah move quickly to put a little distance between her and the danger, and then he returned to the action.

Either the three gunslingers, including Hannah's mother, were terrible shots, or none intended to hit their targets. So far, there appeared to be no gunshot injuries – I saw no blood – though I hoped Tom and Rachel were feeling some pain from being shoved to the floor. Now, with six men and one woman against two thugs – I liked those odds – I figured, what could go wrong? I rushed back down the aisle in search of Billy and Ella. The woman Hannah called Mom remained in the aisle holding a gun in one hand and a cell phone to her ear with the other.

"Have you seen the kids?" I asked.

"They went that way crawling on all fours," she said as she pointed toward one of the side doors and then resumed her phone conversation.

Now I was terrified. Two young ones on their own while a crime involving guns was in progress? Definitely not good. I dashed toward the door.

As soon as I got outside, I heard the sound of one of the jet's engines running, ready for takeoff. Then I looked in all directions for the kids, my heart pounding. What if Tom and Rachel had their own men in black ready to be back-up for their deadly deeds? Even if they couldn't force Hannah, Trace, and Troy to that ready-to-take-off jet, would they use it for own their getaway?

My heart stopped when I saw Billy and Ella standing in the small jet's doorway, the worst place possible. I ran toward them in my long formal gown and heels as if competing for Olympic gold. "Get out of the plane. Now!" I shouted.

I heard another gunshot. Damn! "No, stay where you are." I boarded the jet, insisted the pilot close the door, and prayed we'd be safe for a while.

"I don't know what's going here, but two people held guns to my head and threatened to kill me and my co-pilot – she's also my girlfriend – if I didn't keep the engine running and ready for takeoff until they returned. I was just about to take flight regardless of their threats, but then those little kids came running up, hollering that they needed to get in. I recognized them both from the flight here earlier today, so here they are."

I gave the co-pilot a nod. She was obviously shaken. "We're going to be okay. Nobody's going to get killed." I congratulated the kids for running far away from the *bad guys* but left out that those same people still might try to get on this plane.

"We weren't running away, Mom. We came to get our magic whistles. Remember? I gave one to Ella, and Dad gave one to me."

"He's right," Ella added. "We blew them once, but we should blow them again, so the animals will come and save everybody."

Looking out one of the windows, I saw no sign of anyone coming this way, at least not yet. To make the kids feel better, I asked the pilot if he could open the door for a few seconds. He agreed.

As the magic whistles were blown, we all heard another gunshot.

"Maybe we're too late," Ella cried.

The pilot closed the door and shut down the engine. We all waited, worrying about what would come next. The kids kept busy popping up now and then to look out the window and blow their magic whistles.

"Look at the all pretty lights," Ella said, pointing out the window.

I breathed a sigh of relief as I saw all the red and blue flashing lights surround the lodge. Uniformed officers, some with canines, most with guns drawn, moved cautiously toward the front and side doors. I wished I could have seen everything that transpired up close, but I knew someone would tell me all about it later. For now, I needed to be with Billy and Ella.

We kept the jet's door closed until Trace and Troy arrived in the 8-passenger golf cart and informed us of Tom and Rachel's arrest.

"It's all clear. You can come out and join the others. I do have one question, though. Why are three dogs sitting here by the jet?" Troy asked.

Billy beamed. "We called all the animals with our magic whistles to come and save us. And they did. The dogs were the best. We think a moose walked by, but it didn't stay. We really wanted some buffalo to come closer, but they stayed way back."

Troy whispered in my ear, "Should I tell him they're actually bison, not buffalo?"

Was he joking with me? Either way, my answer was, "No. Definitely not."

CHAPTER TWENTY

HANNAH

The reception got off to a late start due to some police business. I had to give the local law enforcement credit, though. They brought in a forensic crew that scoured in the interior of the building. At the same time, several other officers questioned our guests, some on the patio and others by their official SUV. All those in attendance were spending the night, so no one was in a hurry. Fortunately, Tom and Rachel had already been taken away.

We managed to smile for the cameras as we stood greeting our short line of guests. Not wanting yellow crime tape in our wedding photos, the reception was relocated to the far side of the tent and the tables that were set up for dinner. We were happy to be married, and the wedding ceremony was beautiful, but the past hour had drained us all of energy and any sort of peaceful, easy feelings we might have had.

The musical trio entertained our guests while fancy finger food was served and champagne flowed. The four of us decided to take a needed break and went up to our rooms before joining the others for dinner. Ivy and I soon learned that our men had reserved not only the area where the ceremony took place but also the entire upstairs of this log mansion just for the four of us. It consisted of two huge suites with an even larger living space between them and incredible views in every direction. I didn't mind seeing the buffalo roaming from this vantage point. I enjoyed it.

"What a busy day, huh?" Trace stated the obvious. "You took the surprise well."

"Which surprise? There were several." I had just enough energy left to tease him.

"The wedding Troy and I planned, but let me back up. When I saw the look on your face when you witnessed the damage and every inch of that beautiful little chapel covered in spray paint, it broke my heart. Troy's too."

"Trace is correct. You gals canceled the wedding, which made sense in the moment, knowing how physically and mentally exhausted you both were."

Ivy and I nodded. What they'd said so far was true.

"So, we planned a surprise wedding to make it completely stress-free for you." Trace grinned and then added, "All you had to do was show up."

"We had a little help from Saige and Alice, but Trace wasn't sure how our big surprise would be received," Troy said. "That's when we came up with a back-up plan."

I know my face formed a frown, but my gut wanted to giggle. "A wedding with a back-up plan? Who does that?"

"Two men with an ambitious goal, that's who," Trace said. "If your hands went to your hips, Hannah, and Ivy's foot started tapping, we'd say it was a joke, just dinner – not a wedding."

Now, Ivy's foot did tap, and my hands were on my hips. Seeing the men's faces, we couldn't keep from laughing. Trace grinned, Troy winked, and we all hugged.

Knowing that the guests were spending the night here, I assumed we were too, but that brought another question to mind. Rather than ask it, I excused myself for a few minutes and went to the suite Trace and I would stay in. I breathed a sigh of relief when I noticed a set of luggage and clothes hanging in the closet. There were clothes in the drawers too. I might be able to relax now.

I glanced in the bathroom and then stepped all the way in. Not much rustic, western décor; it was more like an ultra-modern spa. I studied myself in the mirror, mirror on the wall. Though not the fairest of them all, I looked pretty good considering all that had transpired today. I took advantage of the set of wintergreen and lavender lotion and cologne sitting on the counter. Surrounded by the lovely scent, I returned to the group with an idea.

"The wonderful ceremony aside, let's debrief a bit," I said.

Ivy jumped right in with a question. "The black-tuxe-doed doormen weren't really doormen, were they?"

Trace and Troy exchanged glances before saying, "Nope."

"More info would be nice." I helped out Ivy.

"Okay," Troy said. "Kitchi anticipated trouble – a gut feeling – and took it upon himself to hire some extra muscle, more than the doormen, just in case. We didn't know of this until today."

"Who are they, and where did they come from?" Ivy asked.

As it turned out, our men didn't have the answer because all Kitchi had told them was, "I've got people."

"Where are these people now?" All I ever saw were the doormen, but then I was a bit blown away by the entire wedding situation even before Tom and Rachel burst in.

"Everywhere, I assumed, though mostly out of sight looking like groundsmen, hikers, or wedding staff," Troy said. "I think a few were assigned to moose and buffalo duty. They're all on the clock until we head home."

Our discussion moved on. That's when it dawned on me that I hadn't seen Clint since the commotion calmed down and Tom and Rachel were taken into custody.

"Where is Clint?" I asked.

"He'll be fine, Hannah," Troy said.

"That's good news, but it's not a sufficient answer, Troy," Ivy said.

"All right. He's still in the ambulance."

Shocked and worried, Ivy and I said, "What? We need the whole story, Troy."

"One of the bullets grazed his leg. Due to his paralysis, it took him a while to realize what had happened. He's feeling no pain. Really. He refused to be taken to a hospital, and because it was just a flesh wound and he doesn't need stitches, the EMTs are patching him up."

Troy didn't sound worried, so I felt good about Clint's recovery too. Ivy didn't look as convinced. She said, "I wish I could have been the one to patch him up. In a way, I miss my old job."

Trace added, "You know, I think Dad almost enjoyed

getting shot. When they put him on a gurney to carry him to the ambulance, he said, 'Happy to take one for the McAllister team.'"

The McAllister team. I liked the sound of that. I was part of that team now. Hannah McAllister. That sounded even better. I stood, needing to walk around. There were windows on both the east and the west side of the sitting room we were in. Looking to the west, I could see our guests below enjoying the magnificent scenery: the rugged peaks of the Tetons, the pine forests, and the nearby meadows filled with wildflowers. I noticed Ella standing by Lester. Hmm. I was surprised Billy wasn't there with her. Those two were like peas in a pod.

"Hannah, I'm getting a cold drink from the minibar. You want one too?" Ivy asked.

"Sure. Thanks. See if there's a Coke. For some reason, I'm craving one right now."

We stood together at one of the windows, sipping our drinks and watching the wild animals off in the distance. We rejoined our men – the McAllister brothers – on the huge, overstuffed sofas a few minutes later. I think we were finally relaxing. At least I know I was, though my mind still drifted back to our unusual past.

Revelations were unveiled, one after another. A lingering mystery had come full circle today. We had correctly ruled out the culprits of the ongoing vandalism we'd experienced over the past year. During brainstorming sessions, others were eliminated due to incarceration or their own demise. Then came the threatening letters and the horrific vandalism that took place at our newly gifted Wyoming ranch. Still, we hadn't been able to think of anyone else.

"A penny for your thoughts," Trace said, patting my hand.

Then it hit me, and I sprang to my feet. "No! My thoughts are priceless. I should have solved the mystery of notes, letters, and destruction at the cabin in Wyoming the day we looked at the photos on the game camera." I began to tremble.

"Hannah, what's the matter? Talk to me, darlin'." Trace knew I was strong, but I had a delicate side too.

"I'm okay. It's just that I'm reliving the day I was kidnapped and remembering—"

Trace quickly wrapped his arms around me and whispered into my ear, "Breathe, darlin', slow and easy. Did we overlook something?"

"No, not we. Me. This was my mistake. I missed an important telltale clue, one you couldn't possibly know about. That fall day when Rudy kidnapped me, he wore a mask just like the ones the people wore in the game camera photos after the chapel had been ruined – the same kind of masks Tom and Rachel wore today."

I stopped shaking and sat back down. Ivy brought me some water, and Trace never left my side.

"Our toughest, most dangerous mystery began first at The Lucky Seven and ended here today," I said, knowing more details would need to be added.

Troy and Ivy were aware of my friend, Rick, the man I traveled with from Phoenix to Stillwater, Colorado. We were going to share, as friends, a small ranch there named The Lucky Seven.

Trace added his understanding of the bizarre situation. "As it turned out, Rick had a ruthless, maladjusted twin brother named Rudy who, apparently, was raised by twisted and evil foster parents. We had no idea of Tom and Rachel's existence and connection to Rudy until we all met today. Now, I bet they were the masterminds plotting to steal Hannah's lottery winnings right from the start using Rudy as the puppet who would take all the risks."

Troy sat silently, listening and taking it all in. "If I understand these details correctly, they showed up today to avenge Rudy's death and to get your money. Right, Hannah?"

"Yes, it seems that's correct, Troy. There is one last thing I'd like to say on this topic tonight." I felt three sets of curious eyes staring at me. "In Tom and Rachel's minds, we killed their foster son and kept them from acquiring – stealing – millions of dollars from me. So, they were highly motivated. This was an all or nothing crime, and they were willing to take the ultimate risk."

Trace added, "Yes, though incorrectly motivated. They were disturbed, twisted, evil – you name it - and refused to accept the fact that Rudy died while attempting to murder Hannah and me."

In a way, I felt sorry for Rudy. He must have had an awful life. But I pushed those feelings aside, refusing to let his ghost ruin my wedding day.

CHAPTER TWENTY-ONE

ALICE

I commended my sons for finding the perfect location for this exquisite, intimate wedding. This majestic lodge was surrounded by acres of natural beauty – hardly a building in sight except for several log cabins a good distance away. Earlier, when Clint and I settled into our assigned cabin, I noticed a few land vehicles tucked behind an outbuilding hidden by a dense grove of trees. A nice touch. And now that the official wedding dinner was about to take place, I realized that a perimeter had been set up to keep wandering wildlife from disrupting our evening event. We could see them, but they couldn't reach us. An even nicer touch.

It was as if our little group had the whole world to

ourselves, now that Tom and Rachel had been hauled away, soon to be behind bars. Even so, near silence reigned. The actions of the demonized wedding crashers left a lingering feeling of shock that hovered over us like a heavy storm cloud.

The first course of the wedding dinner would be brought out any minute. Watching for its arrival brought on thoughts of Troy. Though proud of his own ranch and horse breeding business, I was convinced that he enjoyed creating gourmet meals even more. He didn't acquire that talent from me . . . or his father.

The tables were topped with white linen cloths and arranged in the shape of a horseshoe. Right away, I'd noticed eighteen chairs and place settings. Perhaps my math was off, but it seemed to me we needed only seventeen. Had someone backed out at the last minute?

"Here they come, the brides and the grooms," someone from the crowd shouted. Everyone clapped as they approached, and I had the honor of ringing the large, brass dinner bell.

"Hey, Mom," Troy said as soon as I was close enough to hear him. "Don't forget to seat the four of us together, with Billy in the middle."

"Hmm. That's going to be tricky because Billy wants to sit by Ella."

We briefly discussed a new seating arrangement, one

I disapproved of. I put on a weak smile to cover my frustration and said, "Sit wherever you want to." And they did.

As it turned out, there may have been an empty chair on purpose – my math was correct after all – but now it was located at the very head and center of the horseshoe-shaped table. My next thought? Did an empty chair at the wedding dinner table mean the same as the riderless horse at a funeral? Did someone die? I shook that thought right out of my head.

As we all stood behind our chairs waiting to be seated, Kitchi asked for a moment of silence before giving the blessing. When he concluded blessing the sky, the earth, all things in nature, and everyone present, a few of the guests said, "Amen," and the copper-colored sun slipped behind the rugged mountainous horizon.

Strings of white lights twinkled in the gray of dusk, and salad plates, each containing an entire head of butter lettuce with a scoop of cold lobster salad in the center, were set in front of each guest.

"Grandma," Billy said. "How do I eat this? It's so big."

"Ask your dad. He created the entire menu." I didn't cringe when he called me grandma. That was a first. Referring to my son Troy as Billy's dad was even more shocking. I got up and whispered into Billy's ear, "Eat the lobster that's in the middle using your little fork, then pick at the lettuce leaves with your fingers. That's what I'm going to do."

Billy reached up and put his arms around my neck. "You're the best grandma ever. Can I tell you a secret?"

"Sure."

"I got real close to a buffalo today."

Flustered, I had no words. I merely pointed at his plate and said, "Eat."

No one noticed our little conversation because they were all staring at an SUV speeding recklessly down The Hideaway Inn's dirt road. Now I was watching the vehicle too as it kicked up dirt until it veered off and parked on the grassy meadow. My sons looked perplexed. Something was about to happen that neither of them expected. Good grief. What now?

Trace and Troy stood up quickly, nearly knocking over their chairs as two people ran toward the group. After all that had transpired during the wedding recessional, I held my breath with cautious anticipation. I noticed several of the guests had that deer-in-the-headlights look in their eyes.

"Sorry I'm late," the woman yelled from a distance.

"Jane! You made it. I was getting worried and didn't like seeing that empty chair over there," Trace said.

I needed answers. "Jane? The sheriff in your neck of the woods, Trace?"

He nodded. His infectious grin set the tone. "Yes, Mom. Now everyone is here."

"Look who I found with a little help from a detective friend of mine," Jane said, smiling as if she'd just discovered buried treasure.

Most of the guests didn't know Sheriff Jane, and I'd met her only once at the Big Mack when we'd celebrated the successful search and rescue when Trace and Hannah were missing.

First, we had one too many chairs. Now, we're short a seat. "Troy, we need another chair, another place setting, and one more ridiculously large salad," I said. If I had feathers, they be ruffled right now.

"I'm on it, Mom."

"You didn't need to run from your SUV to the table, you know," Trace said, giving Jane a hug.

"Running was not my idea; it was his," Jane said, looking pleased with herself and pointing at her companion.

I watched and listened, still unsure of what was going on. Most of the guests kept eating their salads – not as curious as I was – but with the afternoon we'd just spent together, I'd bet money on the fact that they were ready to hide under the table.

This man who Jane brought looked a bit young to be her guy or her date. My questions mounted up. Why would she bring a stranger to this wedding? And how come I didn't know about this extra guest?

"Trace, I'd like you to meet Oakley, Ivy's brother," Jane said. "Oakley, this is Trace, Hannah's husband."

Hearing that name, Ivy turned to look. "Oakley? Oakley! Oh, my God!" She rose from her seat as if in a trance and spoke his name again. "Oakley. Is that really you?"

"It's me," he said, smiling from the opposite side of the horseshoe-shaped table.

Troy was back with the salad. In a flash, he handed it to Trace and was by Ivy's side, offering support. Some guests kept eating; others just stared, not understanding what was happening. I was part of the clueless group.

"Troy, this is my long-lost brother," Ivy said, wiping tears from her eyes.

"Then I suggest," he said, kissing her forehead, "you go give him a hug."

She seemed to be in shock, but I saw her nod and then run toward her brother, where he stood with open arms. Their embrace was a long one.

"You've changed so much Oakley and . . . you're running?"

"Yes, been winning races too."

"It's been so long. We have a lot of catching up to do."

Ivy turned and spoke to the group. "Hey everyone, I'd like you to meet my brother, Oaklcy." Everyone cheered. "We haven't seen each other for eleven years."

Then, softly, she said, "I tried to call you, but your phone was disconnected. And I couldn't find a new number."

"And I had no idea where you were, Ivy, or what you were doing with your life. Figured you didn't want to be found."

"Well, here we are, thanks to Jane. The last time we were together, you couldn't walk, let alone run. And here you are near Jackson Hole without a walker or a wheel-chair running across a meadow and attending my wedding dinner."

Oakley hugged Ivy again and said, "Miracles do happen, little sister, and the medical community has made major strides in the area of prosthetics. Want to see?"

"Uh, no. Not right now. The wedding dinner has already begun."

At least I'm not the only one feeling a bit of shock and awe. I walked toward Oakley and Ivy and held out my hand to him. "Welcome, Oakley. I'm Alice, mother of the grooms." I liked this man from the moment I laid eyes on him. Imagine that. "Tell me, were you named after the overpriced glasses or the tree?" I laughed at myself. "Oh, never mind, I need to rearrange a few guests so you can sit next to your sister."

"Thank you, Alice. By the way, I go by Lee now. Never liked the name Oakley."

I nodded and then smiled when I saw Billy heading over to Ivy and her brother. He'd been quiet for a while.

"Mommy, can I sit by my brother?"

This ought to be good. A chuckle threatened to escape my throat.

"Yes, you can sit here, sweetie, but you don't have a brother. He's . . . he's kind of your uncle."

"You have a child?" Lee asked.

"It's a long story, Oakley."

"Please. Call me Lee."

"I'll work on that." Ivy gazed at her long-lost brother with a look mixed with shock and happiness. "Our piled-high dinner plates will be here any minute. We can talk more later. Right now, I don't have adequate words to describe my feelings. I'm . . . I'm just so happy to see you."

Yes, the sudden appearance of Ivy's brother was a bit shocking. I had one more nagging question to ask Jane privately. Of course, we were never close – I'm not close with anyone, except for Clint, and that's got to change. I hope she's willing to tell me more about how she found Ivy's brother before this day is over.

"Mom," Trace motioned for me to come closer. "While you're rearranging the seating, see if you can place Jane next to Lillian. They have a few things in common, and I think they'll enjoy each other's company."

Interesting. Now I had another question and more work to do. The well-orchestrated dinner had become chaotic. Some guests stood, others sat, all chattering at once. I wasn't sure how to go about making seating changes, so I decided to just do it all at once.

"I'm declaring a dinner intermission," I nearly shouted. "Everyone, on your feet, please, while we rearrange the seating and reset the table for the main course."

The band was on a break, but when Trace asked them to play a few extra tunes during this unplanned pause in the wedding dinner, they agreed. I don't know what Trace actually said to the musicians. However, after he walked away, the tunes they played were beautiful and serene.

After some shuffling by the resort staff and me, we added new place settings and the main entrées. Finally, everyone was seated, happy, and enjoying their dinner.

Using Troy's recipe, the chef prepared beef bourguignon

for the main course and a special version of that for Billy and Ella. Their dinner consisted of tiny, pre-cut pieces of beef atop a generous helping of mac 'n' cheese – white cheese.

Guests avoided comments about all the previous excitement but had plenty to say about the food.

"Best beef bourguignon I've ever had."

"Mm, mm. This meat is so tender it melts in your mouth."

Billy looked up, frowning as he contributed in his two cents. "There's something wrong with my meat. It's not melting in my mouth. Not even a little."

"Your meat is just fine, Billy," I said. "Everyone here is chewing their meat, just like you are." Sometimes, this little guy thinks too much, though I had to admit he was growing on me.

When the server set Hannah's plate down, I noticed a look of distress on her face. Then I remembered, she was the gal who didn't eat meat. Oh, dear. Still, after Trace whispered something into her ear, she dug right in. Interesting. I wonder what he said to her.

Ivy

TWO SERVERS APPEARED. Each held two bottles: one filled with champagne, the other sparkling water. Troy and

Clint requested sparkling water, as I knew they would. The kids were not given a choice, though I doubt they realized that fact. They held up their champagne flutes like all the others.

Once everyone's glass was filled, Alice said, "Let the toasts begin."

Hannah went first. "I'd like to toast our mother-in-law. Alice, here's to you for all your help making our surprise wedding wonderful."

"Hear! Hear!" the guests shouted.

Upon hearing Hannah's toast to Alice, I noticed that Trace grinned and Troy winked – no surprise there. But I didn't know why it brought out the guys' trademark reactions.

Several comments – not official toasts – were shouted out from the seated guests.

"One too many wedding surprises, though!" Muffled laughter followed that one.

I chimed in. "As a soon-to-be author, I could not have written a more shocking ending."

Troy whispered close to my ear, "Your calendar is quickly filling up, my love. Caring for Billy, our Montana animals, your new ranch project, writing a novel, not to mention loving your new husband. Well, let's just say your dance card is full too."

Alice raised her glass and asked for everyone's attention. "I have a wish for my sons and their wives, and I pray it comes true. May they have long, happy, healthy lives with far less drama." The silence was deafening . . . until Alice gave way with a hearty laugh. The others joined in.

Troy stood, raised his sparkling water-filled flute, and spoke so all could hear. "To Mrs. McAllister, my beautiful, talented, and brave wife. I am the happiest man in the world because of you, babe."

"Cheers!"

Apparently, Troy's words sparked a few thoughts compelling Trace to speak. "Troy, do you mind sharing the 'happiest man in the world' title?"

"I suppose that's okay."

"Good! Now, for my toast to my beloved wife, Hannah. I love you more every minute of every day, darlin'. I've been a better man since you came into my life. You're a smart, lovely, horse-whispering woman. I'll love you to the moon and back, forever. But . . . I still can't swallow a hunk of tofu. Hope you can live with that."

The onlookers laughed. Hannah took Trace's face in her hands and kissed his mouth slowly, passionately.

"I think someone should make a movie of this McAllister wedding," Lee said. "And I want to be in it. All in favor?"

"Aye!" was the group's enthusiastic reply. Pretty sure my jaw dropped after hearing Lee's words. I'd never seen him happy before, and apparently, he had more to say.

"To all the future movie stars present at this unique, wild wedding," he continued.

The hear, hears were mixed with laughter, and most of the day's tension floated away.

Clint raised his glass. "To my new daughters, Hannah and Ivy. May their lives be filled with joy, horses, and a lifetime of adventure with my sons, of course. Welcome to the McAllister family. Cheers to you both. Oh, just one more thing. How are your plans for your Wyoming property coming along?"

I looked at Hannah skeptically. Did we want to share what we'd talked about earlier today? We shrugged. Nothing was in stone yet, but we had begun the naming process as well as the purpose of our new ranch. After we nodded, I motioned for Hannah to come stand by me.

"You first, Hannah."

"It's true we'd put our project on hold. But now that our main, dangerous roadblock has been identified and eliminated, it no longer seems so daunting or difficult."

"That's right. We're ready to place the ranch project back on our list of important things to do, and we've settled on a few details," I said. "Mainly, its name and how the property would be used."

We'd keep the information to a minimum because some of our guests knew nothing of our previous plans or difficulties.

"We will have therapy horses, maybe dogs too, gardens, and a small staff," I said. "All would be there to support humans needing emotional or physical therapy. We will also have a special area for animals in need of therapy or sanctuary."

"I think another toast is in order," Hannah said.

"Sure, why not? Let's do it."

"Raise your glasses, everyone," she said as she raised her champagne flute in the air. "Here's to the future development of the MMO."

Cheers were said, although weakly and sounding more like questions. Who could blame them? Our project was multi-dimensional and complicated. Hannah and I looked at each other intensely.

"Ready?" she asked.

"Not quite." I turned and hollered at the band. "A drum roll, please." They obliged immediately, so I said, "Our ranch project has a name." Then Hannah and I spoke the words as one voice. "The Many Miracles Outpost. The MMO!"

Real cheers, loud and enthusiastic, filled the chilly night air.

EPILOGUE

ALICE

I had to admit, this was a spectacular wedding. Everything – except for Tom and Rachel's threats and all that drama – was magnificent right down to the multi-layered, multi-flavored cake. A chocolate layer with raspberry frosting for Ivy, a spiced apple layer with caramel frosting for Hannah, and a strawberry layer with banana mousse frosting for Billy. I'm sure Ella liked that too. The cake was so huge that everyone had a slice of each.

With the moon shining brightly and the strings of small white lights twinkling, Clint and I watched our sons having the last dance with their wives. Most of the guests had retired to their cabins for the night. Billy got to have a sleep-over with Lester and Ella. Kitchi and Saige were the last to head to their cabins. Oh, wait. Are they holding hands? No, the moonlight is playing tricks with my eyesight. I blinked to clear my vision and took another look. Oh, my. They both went into the same cabin. No tricks there. Interesting.

"Dad, do you want us to escort you and Mom back to your cabin?" Trace asked.

"I got this, son. We're going to head that way right now."

All six McAllisters hugged and said good night. Troy was the last one to hug me. With his arms still around me, I whispered into his ear, "I'll begin planning for a nursery, maybe two, just as soon as I get home."

I stifled a giggle seeing Troy's eyebrows raise and his head shake in the moonlight. He whispered back. "No, Mom. We have Billy. He's a kid, not a baby. And, besides, the doctor told Ivy she was unable to have children."

I reached up, held my son's face, and looked into his eyes. "Well, Troy, that doctor was wrong. I know these things." Then, with a lilt in my voice, I said, "Enjoy your wedding night."

I giggled silently, wondering if or when Troy would

figure out what I was talking about. Tonight, feeling that all was right with the McAllisters' world once again, Clint and I headed off into the darkness.

AUTHOR'S NOTE

Having grown up in the mountains of Colorado, five miles from the nearest small town, I learned to love the solitude and the vast wilderness the great outdoors provided. At the time, I had no idea that I would become a writer or how much influence my childhood environment would affect my writing.

After completing Book 3, **Wyoming Sundown**, I realized that I'd set up the need for a wedding or two to take place in the next book. That wasn't my original intention, but that is what happened. However, a story about two engaged couples getting married seemed ordinary, plain, and not that exciting. How would I add mystery, danger, love, and laughter (I always need laughter) to this seemingly simple premise? That was my big challenge. I decided to feature the McAllister women and let them tell their story.

I discovered – only after I've finished writing a story – that I tend to include topics, some tiny, others more significant, from my own past. I'll include a few that come to mind today as I write this note to you.

I have just one brother, a brilliant, wonderful man. Always thought it would be nice to have a sister, but that was not to be. The gals in the story, Hannah and Ivy, have their ups and downs but, eventually, feel as if they are sisters. I consider my real-life sister-in-law to be my sister, now. We don't speak the "in-law" part anymore.

Oatie, Trace's dog in every McAllister Brothers book so far, had the same medical problem and surgery as my own dog, Charlie, a cattle dog. My Charlie died just as I was finishing book 1, COLORADO TAKEDOWN. I feel I must end this series before Oatie passes away. I can't survive that sadness again in real life or in fiction. I do have plans for Book 5, though, and Oatie will be there.

Assuming you've already read **Wild Weddings** (and maybe the first three books in this series, too,) you know that Troy is quite the chef. I enjoyed thinking about scrumptious meals cooked by a hunky cowboy. However, for me, the joy of cooking came late in life. As a child, I was raised on uncomplicated meals. Breakfast consisted of cold cereal and orange juice; Lunch was a bologna sandwich on white Wonder Bread (I may have just given away my age) and an apple; Our dinner plates often held a small baked potato, peas or corn, and a ground beef patty.

After leaving home, I became a fairly decent cook. And, just so you know, I've prepared and eaten most of the meals mentioned in my novels, and sometimes, I include an original recipe or two at the end. Do you have a favorite meal to prepare or partake in?

My parents lived in Sheridan, Wyoming while I was attending college in Greeley, Colorado. To visit them, I'd fly from Denver to Sheridan. The plane made many stops along the way. Frequent passengers called it "a milk run." We were always going up or coming down, never cruising at a comfortable altitude. Several times, due to fog, the plane could not land in Sheridan, and it flew on to Billings. It was always an adventure. An unusual airplane ride comes up in several McAllister Brothers books.

I hope you enjoyed the McAllister women's story. If so, you're invited to join my monthly newsletter so we can keep in touch, and you'll hear about new releases, giveaways, and exclusive content. As of this writing, all I know is that Book 5 will include many Miracles. See you there.

Cricket

What? You missed Book 1 or Book 2 or Book 3?
No worries. It's not too late to catch up.

COLORADO TAKEDOWN

Book 1 in The McAllister Brothers Series

A vegetarian from the city and a cattle-raising rancher
sounds like a match made in hell. But what if they need
each other more than they realize?

How will Hannah deal with becoming a novice rancher
and a fake widow all in one day?

MONTANA COUNTDOWN

Book 2 in The McAllister Brothers Series

Troy, a wealthy rancher and Ivy, a beautiful, would-be
novelist team up

to save the ranch from unthinkable evil and end up
fighting for their lives. It seemed the end was near when
an unexpected visitor shocked them all.

WYOMING SUNDOWN

Book 3 in The McAllister Brothers Series

Trace and Troy agree to take their dad's challenge and
ride horseback across the remote wastelands of Wyoming
with Christmas just weeks away.

Three men in danger, three women worry. What could possibly go wrong?

CLOVER

The horse, Clover, is Kitchi's horse in WILD WEDDINGS and was inspired by the real horse Miranda de Dragoon. She's from a genetically important, critically rare heritage breed called The Wilbur-Cruce Mission Horse, part of a larger group known as Spanish Barbs.

BEAUTY

Beauty is one of Trace's horses in WILD WEDDINGS.
Her character was modeled after the real horse, the
beautiful chestnut mare Julietta de Dragoon, also a
Spanish Barb owned and trained by Jerry Gallegos.

CLOVER / MIRANDA & BEAUTY / JULIETTA
(mother & daughter)

Photo by Alana Carden

Julietta – born approximately eight years ago near the Dragoon Mountains in southern Arizona – was the "surprise" baby of Miranda.

The Spanish Barb Horse Association (SBHA), formerly known as the Spanish Barb Breeders Association (SBBA) is dedicated to the preservation, perpetuation, and promotion of the Spanish Barb Horse. They have changed their name but not their mission. The Spanish horse was made to build the West, and that it did!

You can learn more about this amazing breed at the following locations:

www.spanishbarb.com

https://www.facebook.com/groups/130122983703371/

THANK YOU!

Thank you for reading *Wild Weddings*.

Would you like to know when the next book in the *McAllister Brothers* series is available? That's easy. Sign up for Cricket's (almost) monthly NEWSLETTER and you'll receive notifications of new books, giveaways, and other exclusive content.

If you enjoyed this story, please leave a REVIEW on Goodreads, Bookbub, or your favorite online retailer. Reviews are helpful to readers and appreciated by authors

ABOUT THE AUTHOR

Cricket grew up in Estes Park, Colorado, and spent her formative years among deer, coyotes, and beautiful blue columbine. Living on the boundary line of the Rocky Mountain National Park, she could wander in by merely stepping out the backdoor.

Today Cricket is a full-time author writing Sweet Romance, Westerns, Women's Fiction, and Romantic

Mysteries about cowboys, teachers, the great outdoors—even Alzheimer's. So far, there is a delightful dog in each of her novels.

Before heading down the mountain to attend college in Greeley, Colorado, Cricket took up playing the guitar and sang with her brilliant brother's folk group, The Sundowners, later called Friendship Sloop. During these singing years, she was bitten by the show-biz bug and appeared in TV pilots, numerous commercials, and theatrical voice-overs.

Cricket loves to hear from readers.
Connect with her via:

Website https://www.cricketrohman.org

Facebook https://facebook.com/CricketRohmanAuthor

Twitter https://twitter.com/CricketRohman

Bookbub https://www.bookbub.com/authors/cricket-rohman

www.goodreads.com/author/show/112683.Cricket_Rohman

Email cricketrohman@gmail.com

WANT MORE?

You will find the links and excerpts for all of Cricket
Rohman's books HERE and/or www.cricketrohman.org

The McAllister Brothers Series
Romantic Western Adventures

COLORADO TAKEDOWN, Book 1
This twisty cowboy adventure includes treachery, new love, family, courage, and amazing ranch animals.

MONTANA COUNTDOWN, Book 2
A wealthy rancher's story-telling tendency entices two eavesdroppers—a greedy criminal and a would-be novelist—to venture to his Montana ranch to search for his hidden treasure.

WYOMING SUNDOWN, Book 3
Clint McAllister's challenge put his sons in grave danger. Alice is furious about his foolish plan. It was almost Christmas, a bad time for such nonsense.

WILD WEDDINGS, Book 4
Family, fate, and formidable danger make loving and laughing a challenge. Trace and Troy love two city gals. Their love is strong but their plan for new ranches and happy lives is threatened at every turn. Who wishes them harm?

The Creative Hearts Sweet Romance Series
Creative Women Standalone Novellas

PHOEBE'S PHOTO FETISH
Phoebe Foxglove had three loves: Photography, Flowers, and Bobby.
Two out of the three served her well.

TINA'S TASTY TOURS
Tina has an impossible dream that comes with a substantial price tag. In the meantime, she works at the Punk Patio and a 1960s diner where she is required to look like Marilyn Monroe.

The Lindsey Lark Series
Fiction with Elements of Romance & Mystery

WANTED: AN HONEST MAN
Lindsey, a kinder teacher in survival mode after an unthinkable divorce, is brilliant in the classroom. Unfortunately, unwanted sinister challenges invade her off-hours.

LETTERS, LOVERS, & LIES

Jake and Lindsey are in love, but so much stands in their way. Fortunately, they are smart, multi-talented, and they love to laugh. Wendell, the 180-pound lovable mastiff, is featured throughout this series.

HIT THE ROAD, JAKE!

Thrilling, romantic, and sprinkled with humor, this novel reinvents the 'buddy movie' concept with the written word… and a pretty woman. As Jake and Lindsey travel from Tucson to Estes Park in their RV, the dangers they face become deadly.

The Fantasy Maker Series
Contemporary Adventures

FOREVER ISLAND

JD won a contest and ended up on a deserted island somewhere in Micronesia.
This is a wild beach adventure complete with danger, love, and a dog named Noodles.

WINTER'S BLUSH

The Fantasy Maker strikes an agreement with Clay.

What's the catch? He must pretend to be someone he's not. A quick read that includes mountain hiking, rescue dogs, danger, and yes, some romance.

Saving Madeline

Standalone Contemporary Fiction

An entertaining story with humor, emotion, and an unusual mother-daughter relationship.

Christmas in the North Woods

A Children's Picture Book

Oliver Owl introduces the reader to his forest friends who are busy rehearsing for the annual Christmas Song Contest.